ALSO BY SUSAN ENGBERG

Pastorale
A Stay by the River

SARAH'S LAUGHTER

AND OTHER STORIES

SARAH'S LAUGHTER

AND OTHER STORIES

by Susan Engberg

ALFRED A. KNOPF   NEW YORK   1991

THIS IS A BORZOI BOOK
PUBLISHED BY ALFRED A. KNOPF, INC.

Copyright © 1991 by Susan Engberg

This work was supported in part by a grant
from the National Endowment for the Arts.

Library of Congress Cataloging-in-Publication Data
Engberg, Susan.
Sarah's laughter and other stories / by Susan Engberg.—1st ed.
p.   cm.
ISBN 0-394-58556-9
I. Title.
PS3555.N387S27   1992
813'.54—dc20   91-52734
CIP

Manufactured in the United States of America

First Edition

With love and gratitude
to my father, King, and in memory of my mother, Julia
and to Charles, Siri, and Gillian

CONTENTS

Sarah's Laughter

AND OTHER STORIES

SARAH'S LAUGHTER

I

Dressed in old seersucker and a straw hat, Thomas Burden strolled toward her corner. The June day was sweet. During the spring it had become his custom on his afternoon walk to circumambulate the small green neighborhood containing Sarah's house, first tracing the outlines of his new state of grace—the streets of heavier traffic, scant shade, shops, restaurants, and apartment buildings made a framework for his musings—before turning in beneath the trees of Olive Street to approach what he believed to be the center of it: Sarah herself or, rather, their renewed friendship, their forgiveness, more or less, of each other after almost twenty years.

He came to the brick wall, the herringbone-patterned brick walk by the glossy euonymus vines, then the roofed passageway to her door, all of this a carefully planned progression from urban to private, but there to his left the high wooden gate to the courtyard was conspicuously ajar and inside beneath the young sycamore tree dozed a defenseless Sarah. Alarm fluttered up in him. Anyone could have wandered up from the street and been stopped, as he was now, by the sight of a white-haired woman, her chin fallen to her chest, her cane hooked on the back of her chair, her knees slightly splayed, her feet in thick walking sandals. Not even the red setter was with her. Anyone could have stolen in and done swift damage. It was lucky the one to have come along was he, who above all now wanted to keep harm outside their newly defined pale. Even before, when he had been her husband, though perhaps less consciously her friend, he had never for a moment, he assured himself, meant harm.

He stepped into the walled court and pushed the gate gently until it clicked shut. She lifted her head. "Hello, Thomas," she said. Concern over her lack of precaution almost outweighed the pleasure he took in her accessibility. Her napping alone with the gate open was certainly not what her present husband would have had in mind when he had conferred with the architect about "hierarchies of organization" and "buffer zones" and "inner sanctums."

Thomas took a chair near her and rested his hat on his knee. "Hello, Sarah." She was Sarah Hardt now, and Thomas knew about Otto Hardt's conversations with the architect from Otto himself, who had become his friend also and part of the miracle. "Otto is a capital fellow," Thomas had offered in conversation with others, those few others with whom he still conversed. To Sarah one day not long ago he had said in an uneven voice, "We're just three old people now, aren't we?" and she had laid her hand on his knee because it had been impossible for him to say any more.

"Have you had your walk yet?" he asked.

"Not yet. I'll take a turn with you now, if you'd like." This little exchange, with variations, was almost a ritual now.

"I'd always like," said Thomas. He took up her hand and brought it to his lips. Certain gestures had also come within the bounds of their new ceremonies. It was like learning to dance all over again, only this time the music was so haunting that it seemed to be coming from a life he could not remember living.

These days he was often reaching up to press a hand on his chest, over his heart.

"I'll get Jesse," said Sarah. "Poor old thing. I thought for sure this warm weather would loosen her hips, but she still appears just as stiff."

Thomas stood as Sarah stood, steadied herself, and made her way to the sliding glass door. She was wearing a loose cotton blouse and a longish full striped skirt, in light shades of gray and tan, and when she emerged again he imagined for an absurd instant that they had just met and his whole life, a different life, was to begin. The setter, Jesse, came slowly after her—Thomas and Sarah had been parted long enough for her to have had a dog grow old—and she was slow herself, with her cane and her injured leg.

The change in their relations had begun in March after her automobile accident. From the hospital, through Otto, she had sent Thomas a request to come to her. This time it was not to discuss their daughter or to tend to any remaining detail from their past marriage, but simply to be with her and to talk: it was time now, she said, high time—indeed, there was no time to lose. In both of them there must already have been some invisible inward clearing of their old material of grievance and bafflement, for in those weeks of his daily visits to the white hospital room they had leapt directly into a clean medium. He did not know how it had happened. They had smiled at each other. It was a new condition, and in it he felt nascent and almost shy.

When he said to her today, "And how is your leg?" he meant: *Here I am next to you on the face of the earth.* And when she answered, "Tolerable," he wished that a new language entirely would spring up to help them in this fresh state of communion.

They walked away from the center of town, on toward the park, not touching, the dog sometimes nosing ahead of them, sometimes behind, while Sarah told him of a telephone call from their only child, Martha, a photographer. She sounded, Sarah related, really exhausted, almost completely strung out.

"In all these years she has never learned how to pace herself," said Sarah.

Thomas's answer, "The rigors of strong-mindedness have always seemed preferable to me to an uncritical comfortableness," was not what he wanted to say.

"Thomas, Thomas," said Sarah, but without the bite of her old exasperation, "I'm only speaking of getting the proper rest." She walked slowly, rhythmically with her cane.

This avenue to the park had changed very little in the half-century Thomas had known it. The two-story frame houses had been built to last, and the trees had never been predominantly the doomed elms. So closely set were the narrow houses that Thomas sometimes pictured them as the partially drawn-out folds of an accordion's bellows: the lined street could then indeed be said to be holding its breath as one age of the world was passing into the next.

Thomas had felt a kind of pride in his daughter when she had confided in him some years ago that she was just trying to live from one shocking month to the next, getting by with as much style as she could muster until the unmerciful end of the whole charade. It shamed him now to recall the awful satisfaction he had taken in Martha's cynicism, but he had been so lonely after the divorce, which had confirmed all his worst opinions of life, that it had been a dark comfort to him to see how much she reminded him of himself.

In the first years of marriage Thomas had not wanted children at all. If it had not been for Sarah's charming determination those nearly forty years ago, this sophisticated child, so different from her mother, would never have been born. For a time, remaining childless had seemed like a point of honor with Thomas, one of the few he had thought still available. He had not sufficient illusions, he had told Sarah, to carry out the job.

But Sarah had smiled at him again and again in such a way

that his point of honor had begun to lose its logic in the face of her sheer, naive, creative power—or whatever her force was to be called—and so with an attempt at humor he had changed his code and said with mock gallantry, "Women and children first." In so many words he had added that if he were generous enough to make possible her motherhood—what he termed to himself her doomed, simplistic, communal gesture—then she would have to allow him eccentricity, complexity—in short, as much individualism as he craved. For he had had a theory in those days that if he could just be allowed to go as far as he was able in his own idiosyncratic direction, staying as unassimilated, as unconventional as he could get away with, then he might just find a way through the indignity of mankind as a body. Without exactly stating it, he had formulated a sort of agreement with Sarah: both of them, he told himself, would follow their "natures," and they would then see what they would see. Time would tell.

Now time was indeed trying to tell—something. Thomas cast a quick, appraising look at Sarah's profile as she turned to call back to Jesse. *We're not done yet,* he wanted to say to her.

"Anyway," said Sarah after she had gotten the dog's attention and had turned back to her measured gait, "Martha says she will come for a visit and a bit of a rest, probably around the Fourth, and I told her we'd take her to the cottage, and then last night Otto and I were talking about how you must be invited to come, too, especially if Martha's time is to be so short. Please think about it, Thomas. It would do you good to get out of that stuffy apartment, and you'd have all those nice hours with Martha out in the boat or whatever."

"Otto is a capital fellow," said Thomas.

"Do you want to know something, Thomas?" She said this calmly, without breaking the rhythm of her walk. "I have never really been able to tell when you are scorning something or when you are valuing it."

Thomas lowered his eyes to his brown, crepe-soled walking

shoes. "I'm afraid I don't express myself very well these days. I value Otto very much. I can see now what he has done for you, and he has been good to me, too."

"Otto is genuinely optimistic. I think that bothers you."

"Otto functions very well—a great deal better than most of us."

"There you go again," said Sarah, but her tone was still amiable.

How, where? he wanted to ask. *I am waiting to know.*

Until his retirement, Thomas Burden had been a newspaperman, in later years the chief of the book section. Thousands of facts and opinions had been squeezed from his mind and tapped out, on schedule, by his fingers. Sacs of fatigue still hung beneath his hooded eyes, and even though he had no more external deadlines, he often raked his fingers hurriedly through his hair. He had a long face, a long body, long hands, long feet, a ranging mind: when he had sat down to work, he had felt as if he were bending himself to the task, folding himself up to fit the desk and the machines and the largely inferior objects of criticism. One book in fifty—no, one in a hundred, maybe in more—might ease his sense of cramp.

"I am sincere in my admiration," said Thomas. "Otto is one in a thousand, one in a million."

"And what am I, dear Thomas?"

"Of you, my dear, I am simply in awe these days. I have no words adequate. I even hesitate to reach out my hand for fear that you will vanish again."

"I never really vanished. I was always here."

"For me, you did." Thomas felt his jaw tightening into an old grimace. Above and ahead of them the trees were lush with new green. Wooden steps spilled down from houses, family houses. He was seventy-seven now: generations had multiplied and spilled down these steps since he and Sarah had kept a house together. The process just kept blindly going on, didn't it? Smells came from some of the houses—of hallways, cellars, food, laundry products. He supposed that there were smells that came from his apartment, too, which he would no longer distinguish because they were too intimate—old man smells. His jaw stayed set. He looked straight ahead through watery eyes.

"Listen to me, Thomas. All of this doesn't need to matter anymore as long as you'll agree to come out regularly and let us all fuss over each other. Do think about coming with us on the Fourth. Especially in summertime you shouldn't be cooped up so much in those little rooms of yours. Why did you insist on moving into such a queer apartment? It has given me such pain to see your lack of concern for your own comfort."

"I've been quite comfortable enough. My apartment is appropriate. I felt it was only right that I should live in reduced circumstances."

Sarah said nothing. She slipped a hand through his arm. In silence they walked the length of another block together, and then Sarah called in the dog and they crossed the last street before the park. At the opening stood several great white oak trees, broad, gnarled, thick with life.

"How would you have had me live?" he asked.

She had stopped and was looking straight into his eyes. "More happily," she said and looped her arm through his. "That has always been the question between us, Thomas, don't you think? I felt that you were mocking me because I wanted life to be pretty and happy."

"Life *isn't* pretty, Sarah," he said habitually, but even as he spoke he thought that he might never have really wanted to be happy or pleasing until that moment.

She shook his arm. "Who told you that?"

"No one needed to tell me that. All I had to do was to look around . . ." After a moment, with what he hoped sounded like dignity he said, "I was trying to be honest with myself."

She shook his arm again, gently, and said, "Thomas."

They walked on, around the area where the small children were at play on the swings and teeter totters and climbing equipment, around the tennis courts.

"Look there," said Sarah, pointing with her cane. "Look at all those young bodies."

"Some day they'll be just like us," he answered.

"If they're lucky," she said and raised her eyebrows at him beneath the loose white waves of hair on her forehead. Her hair had gotten prettier as she had aged. *She* had gotten prettier. Something about her—her beauty? her equanimity?—was making his heart ache. He thought he didn't feel as well as he had when they had started down the avenue, and something in him began withdrawing from her—from her equanimity, her beauty. It was hard for him even to look at her. For an instant the idea came to him that he was jealous, right now, and that jealousy might be what this trouble between them had always been. It seemed impossible. He kept on walking, eyes ahead.

At the narrow river they found an empty bench. Sarah arranged her skirt and lifted and straightened the injured leg, then rotated the foot at the ankle. "See that, Thomas? Improvement." She rested her foot on the stretched-out body of the setter—the dog who knew Thomas as a latter-day visitor. Twenty years it had been since Sarah had left his house. *Twenty years.*

"I don't think the cottage would be a good idea for me," he said suddenly. He had been watching the water, the clouds and trees under the water, the bits of things—leaves, sticks, papers, fallen blossoms—floating on its surface. The cloud images wavered, the trees swayed, the bits rushed and rushed. Even his own vantage point was an illusion of steadiness, but it was all he had. He beat the fist of one hand into the palm of his other. "I'm afraid I'd feel on stage up there. Everything would be too set up, too lit up. I'd turn fractious." He faced her. "You and Otto mustn't try to make a project out of me."

Sarah raised her eyebrows at him again. "I'd say the project is a good deal larger than you, Thomas."

"Why, I think what you're trying to do is set up a commune, Sarah. Admit it. A geriatric, utopian commune. That's no place for an unregenerate like me."

Sarah laughed. "Three or four days of rest and sun simply sound like a vacation to me. Think about it."

"I will consider what Martha has to say," said Thomas with some stiffness, for he had had an image just then of his rooms where, alone these twenty years, his own friend, his own enemy, he had endured his solitary body and his brooding mind; where, persevering, he had now and then in flashes picked up traces of what seemed to be a path he could call his own. Swiftly, like clouds, his old irritation, his old disbelief in Sarah was passing into his vision. Why had he been so foolish of late as to think Sarah had something he needed? Women used men, didn't they? They could drag you down, entice you off your course, make you think that through them you were really going to discover something.

"And just what is your project, Sarah?" he asked. He wondered why Otto was such a fool as to put up with all her maneuverings. He and Otto were the ones who should be getting their heads together, to decide what should be done about *her*. He waited to hear her foolishness.

"You needn't look at me like that, you know," said Sarah. "All I'm trying to set up are a few more chances for us to act a little more in each other's interests. I tried to tell you this in the hospital. Didn't I? Thomas?"

He dropped his eyes to his long hands, dangling between his knees. In these past weeks he had almost forgotten how much she had hurt him years ago, how humiliated he had been. He said nothing.

"What came to me in the hospital was so clear," she continued. "I saw the whole world, and then I saw us—you and Martha and Otto and me—and I saw what it might be like if we all started to live a little more for the sake of each other, if we started to think on a slightly larger scale."

Thomas snorted. He couldn't help himself. They might have been young all over again—and she had always been nine years younger than he—having the same argument all over again. "Altruism is sticky, Sarah. Sticky, sticky." He confronted her, but at the sight of her blue eyes, his irritation became more like anguish. "I don't know if I'm up to being part of your little project," he said more gently. *Be careful,* he wanted to say to her. *Most people, including me, don't behave very well.*

"I'll send Martha over when she arrives, to have a word with you," she answered him. Then she appeared not to be paying much attention to him. With the side of her sandaled foot she was rubbing up and down the back of the setter. Her eyes were intent on the opposite bank, somewhere on the trees that were casting down their reflections.

Thomas picked up a stick from the ground and began breaking it into pieces. "What I'd say is that these little afternoon walks are probably just about the right speed for you and me. More than that and we might end up as we did before."

There was a smile on Sarah's lips, but she didn't turn to him or answer him. The dog Jesse wrinkled her brows and watched them both.

As it turned out, that day was to be the last for several weeks in Thomas's run of good health. By evening all his chronic disgusting and depressing symptoms had returned—the debilitating abdominal pains, the bloat, the diarrhea, the bloody discharge. In addition, he got that night while sleeping a crick in his neck, very painful, which seemed to affect every move he made. He felt stiff and defiled, a shell of pollution. The next day he took taxis to the doctor's office and home and nearly crawled up the walk and the stairs to his apartment.

Years ago he had told himself that his section of town was just seedy enough so that no one in his right mind would ever become so inspired as to attempt major and disrupting overhauls of the old brick buildings. This had suited Thomas. He had burrowed in and stayed, with his oak furniture, his books, his photographs. Voices of other tenants on stairways and fire escapes and in hallways and other apartments he had construed to his rueful amusement as the dramas of folly they no doubt were, and he gave them names as he persevered habitually in his own undoubtedly foolish solo play. He called them: The Bride Bereft, The Adulterer of Limited Means, The Glutton Who Falls Down Stairs, The Widower and the Drinker, Beauty and the Beast, The Ladies Who Come and Go, and, most recently, The Girl Who Needs to Adore. His own drama he called: The Man Who Has Made Too Many Judgments.

For several days Thomas did not even open the Venetian blinds in his apartment. The old air conditioner droned. He lay on the unkempt sheet and dwelt upon his harrowed innards and the pain at the base of his neck just to the right of his spine. In a different age he had been a small child, the son of a mother who had washed and fed and dressed this body. He had been tended. There was a sharp demarcation between this silky memory and all that had happened since.

When Thomas was thirteen, his parents divorced. Puberty had already made it a slippery time for him, and with the absence of his father his confused loneliness increased. He had few friends in that small town. He belonged to himself, he had found, but whoever he was could not exactly be trusted; even now, these thoughts, these physical malfunctions were so much his own, yet so distressingly out of his control. Well, at least his mother had not had to witness the long desecration of her Tommy by temperament and circumstances. Thomas felt his mouth setting itself in the familiar downward grimace of sour endurance.

Sarah telephoned him, and at first he answered her flat on his back, from his habitat of foulness. He surmised that her voice was not to be trusted. Tending him now would be more than enough to try her high ideas: she'd sneak away again, just as she had before, unable to stand him. As he listened to her and answered her plainly and dryly and sometimes perversely, the spring just ending, that brief, gentle, fresh expectancy, now seemed to him an aberration, a trick. Heat had settled in. Gall rose up, and he felt that his long judgment on life was coming back to him, proven.

He passed in and out of unsatisfying sleeps. He went to the bathroom at all hours of the day and night. He drank a little canned soup broth and ate some crackers and a piece of toast. The air was close and fetid, but it was all the air he had. His few possessions did not appear to him charming in the least. Even the photographs on his bedroom wall, most of them of Martha or taken by Martha, did not comfort him, nor the cases crammed with books. With great fatigue and something like shame, he concluded that his work of all those years had been concocted and shallow. And, of course, ephemeral. It was no little joke: he was indeed The Man Who Had Made Too Many Judgments. All his life he had made discriminations, between this and this and this and this, and he had tried to follow himself, but here he was, ending in ignorance and stench.

On the second night the doorbell rang at about a quarter to six. Thinking it was the paperboy making his collection rounds, or Dorie, the young librarian who lived across his landing and had this last year ridiculously fixed upon him, on the basis of a few discussions in the hallway and a few of his books borrowed, as an object of her devotion, he did not answer the persistent ringing. The boy could easily stop again, and heaven knew The Girl Who Needs to Adore did not need any more fuel for her emotions. The bell was pressed again and again, now in a rhythm that sounded like a coded message—an impertinence, Thomas thought. At last in annoyance he got up, tied on a bathrobe, and holding his long, weak body with care, went slowly into the living room, pressed the button and spoke into the intercom.

"It's Otto, Thomas," said a voice ragged with static. He opened the door a crack and waited as footsteps ascended. In the hallway some light filtered down from a dirty skylight onto beige walls and aged red patterned carpeting; in his apartment a little dusty sunlight squeezed around the closed blinds, making scraps of pattern on the faded upholstery and old wood. Thomas leaned his head against the door and closed his eyes.

In a few moments there indeed was Otto, coming up the second flight of stairs with a napkin-covered basket on his arm. "How are you, my fine fellow?" he said to Thomas.

Not fine and not your fellow. Thomas kept his mouth pressed into a frown of forbearance until Otto reached his level, and then he said, "You look accoutered for a charity visit, Otto. Did Sarah put you up to this?"

"Of course she did, but I'm here on my own account, too. How are you feeling?"

"Not at all well. But you might as well come in as long as you've climbed all that way. I'll tell you how I am: abominable, and as weak as a baby. I've been totally reamed out, but what's left is still detestable. Come in, if you've got the stomach for it."

Shuffling, exaggerating his infirmity and the few years of age he had over Otto, he led the way into the stale room. "Sit down," he said. "I've got to sit myself, this instant." He lowered himself over an armchair and then sank into it. He pointed to the basket. "What has our mutual friend been up to?"

"Some dinner," said Otto, "and I have very particular instructions to serve it up to you myself. So why don't you sit where you are, and I'll set up a tray or something. Or a TV table. Do you have a TV table?" Fair-headed Otto was looking around the room, and from below and behind him Thomas was surveying his own shabby cell with the satisfaction of a sufferer: these rooms suited him exactly, he thought, and Otto might as well see the true colors for themselves.

"There should be a tray in the kitchen," said Thomas, gesturing, careful of his neck, "although it might not be possible to find anything in there."

Otto set the covered basket on the oak library table by the window. "May I?" he asked and then manipulated the blinds until the light slanted in, but without glare.

Thomas squinted at the very white napkin that covered the basket and beyond it at the weedlike, luxuriant tree of heaven outside. He thought of it as his tree, a volunteer beneath his window from a crack in the alley—fast-growing, large-leafed, primeval in appearance, maybe a little disgusting if you considered yourself knowledgeable about landscaping. Each year Thomas hoped that it would not be noticed and cut down, and he was careful not to mention the existence of the tree to anyone. At various times of year and at various hours of day and night it cast large-fingered, primitive shadows on the surfaces of his apartment, inside which he was still a creature, no matter the endless convolutions of his thinking.

"This will do dandy," said Otto, returning. On Thomas's lap he set a battered tray, painted with a scene of bookstalls along the Seine, bought ages and ages ago by Thomas and Sarah. "She fixed some things she hoped would agree with you."

With eyes that felt weak and watery, Thomas watched Otto take containers from the basket. Otto was broad-backed, not very tall, with white hair that still held some traces of reddish-blond. His hands were freckled, competent in handling the dishes of food. He had been a widower; he had nursed an invalid wife. He was childless, too. Between the three of them now was one child, Martha—unless Thomas himself was considered by them to be descending into a last puerility. Too weak at the moment to determine whether something was being done to him or for him, Thomas let the food be placed upon his lap. Lids were removed. There were chicken soup with noodles, applesauce, a square of cornbread, and a little container of honey. Otto went to the kitchen again and came back with a cup into which he poured tea from a thermos. Steam rose in the afternoon light. Thomas took a spoonful of the soup. Tears came to his eyes, and his mood softened a little. He chewed and swallowed and took a sip of tea.

"Well?" asked Otto.

"Thank you," said Thomas. "I believe I'll be able to eat some of this. Please, won't you sit down?"

Otto brought up a straight-backed chair and sat with his large, mottled hands on his knees, by all appearances prepared to enjoy the entire meal vicariously. "How's business?" asked Thomas, to deflect some of this eagerness and conserve his own energy for the task of consuming food. Sweat prickled on his forehead; he felt dizzy with weakness and with the effort that was necessary to maintain his life.

"The Davis Street deal is almost sewn up," said Otto. "Did you walk by to see the interior? Good wood there. I'm very pleased." He went on about the structure and the details, and Thomas retreated into a profound eating. His mind was descending into his stomach where he hoped that by some magic his digestion would do a proper and quiet job of transformation on the food.

Otto talked on. A real estate developer of considerable astuteness, he obviously relished recounting his latest alchemy with the arcane elements of property, credit, politics. He was a watcher of neighborhoods. His own present one he had declared to Thomas to be a pocket of civility that would certainly be preserved, anchored as it was by the proximity of the library and court house, the good architecture of the shops and apartment buildings nearby, the park at the far end of the main avenue, the fine old trees.

Thomas put down his spoon and broke into the cornbread. He nodded to Otto and asked about the taxes on the new building, all the while reflecting on this hearty, broad-faced man to whom success adhered, to whom Sarah adhered. So straightforward was Otto that it was almost possible, now, to listen to him without feeling burdened by the past. Years ago, following the divorce and Sarah's remarriage, when Thomas had been in a lowered state that amounted nearly to incapacitation, he had thought narrowly, meanly of Otto's prosperity. It was of an obvious sort, he had concluded: lowbrow, material, tidied up, *pretty*—probably just what the simple, basic Sarah—the Sarah he had tried to inculcate with some hard thinking—had deserved.

At that time Sarah had gone to live in Otto's country house, and for Thomas she had virtually disappeared, involuted with barely a trace. Out in the suburban hills had been ensconced a woman who tended the rose garden of yet another woman, dead, and sent him brief, businesslike messages, sometimes through Martha, of college age then and quickly becoming a woman herself, but Thomas's Sarah—his ideas of a possible Sarah—lost substance. The adversary, the recalcitrant material had vanished. He had not known at what a loss he would be when each day no longer required tactical resistances to her influence. He had not known that he had that much vitality in him to be so full of hurt. His hands had closed upon nothing. His eyes had fastened on the shapes of emptiness. His arguments, his philosophies had dissipated into thin air. Work had become the slit through which he still tried to muster speech, but privately he had made himself alone in the city, abstracted himself as much as possible from its dense texture, let various outer connections attenuate and dissolve, followed instead his own thoughts.

Then several years ago he had heard that Otto was building a house on Olive Street; then the work could be seen to be commenced; then Sarah could be seen occasionally from a distance, or close enough in the streets or in the stores for Thomas and Sarah to exchange a few ordinary words; then the house had been completed, the vines were planted by the brick wall, and the woman in flesh returned to the territory he had claimed for himself through twenty years of solitary peregrination. His imagination, having been harshly emptied and then by strict control held to a semblance of vacancy, as far as this woman was concerned, was again invaded by her solidity; his mind grasped upon her nearness; he began to think what he might say, what she might say, how he might begin all over again to assert and define himself.

And so when her message came from the hospital, he was already primed for dialogue, but the great surprise was that when the actual conversations began, the words he had rehearsed sounded stilted and inadequate. Everything had shifted to a new disposition of coevals. For one thing, he had scarcely taken Otto into account at all, had not figured him in his internal equation. And then suddenly there he was: large, bland, competent, rich, extending to Thomas a friendly hand, at first no doubt because of Sarah, in the emotional press of an accident that had been inches from fatal, and then within weeks apparently because of his own sociable inclinations. Without guile, Otto reaped profits and showered benefits; the stuff of life passed through him unstoppered, perhaps indiscriminately. Here he sat, watching food be consumed, simply wanting to see things go well, to be turned to advantage. The attentions of Otto might or might not be inspired by Thomas himself, personally; it was hard to tell.

Thomas emptied his cup of tea. He had eaten nearly everything. For every word of his own he had received fifty or a hundred from Otto. If at that moment they were to lay their accumulated dollars out on the oak library table, Otto's would outnumber his by fifty or perhaps a hundred to one. And Otto also had Sarah—to the extent to which Sarah could ever be said to be held. And yet Thomas had—what did he have?— something—there must be something. He leaned back gingerly in his chair. Behind Otto's figure, behind the slatted blinds, the tree of heaven splayed out crudely. After the passage of so much time, Thomas could almost look at the situation with detached curiosity: yes, together, he and Otto might make one tolerably complete human male.

He gestured to the empty dishes. "You've done a good deed tonight, my friend. I think you've helped—you and Sarah—to subdue this abominable, beastly flare-up. I'm on the road now, I believe."

Otto began repacking the basket. "Sarah spoke to you about coming along with us to the cottage? You're very welcome, Thomas. It would please us both. And it might be good for Martha, too. I don't know how much Sarah has said to you, but she has been quite worried—well, one thing and another—"

"Thank you," said Thomas, wanting this moment to be over. "I'll see how I progress these next few weeks. And convey my thanks to Sarah. Tell her I cleaned my bowl."

Afterwards, Thomas sat for a long time in his chair. He sat until the tree of heaven lost some of its green to the approaching night and other tenants could be heard coming home. The various sounds of evening had begun. At about eight o'clock he heard a rustling and saw that a folded piece of paper was being slid under his door: a piece of eggshell-blue paper: Dorie, no doubt. He held his breath until the footsteps crossed the hall and a door closed, and then he let out a great, long sigh. The Girl Who Needs to Adore had no idea what sort of hopeless old fart she had chosen. He simply wasn't up to Dorie's notes tonight. He got up from his chair, leaving the blue paper where it was, and stole back to bed. Perhaps he would work himself up to a bath later on or turn on the lights and read or watch television, but for the moment the essential thing was digestion, and it was taking all the concentration he had.

By the middle of the next week, Thomas had walked around the block several times, had eaten six more dinners cooked by Sarah and delivered by Otto, and had received three more notes from Dorie Green, all on stationery of various colors. One early afternoon when he felt he could put her off no longer and when he was sure that she would be at work, Thomas sat down to his desk and reread all the notes, in order.

Dear Professor Burden,

(She knew quite well that he was not a professor, but this name was apparently part of her delusion.)

I have not seen you for several days and so have been unable to tell you the joy I have been experiencing in reading the book of poems you lent me. How could you have known how perfect Yeats would be for me? You know me! I read it every night before I go to sleep. My understanding is following a bird of exaltation.
With heartfelt thanks,
Dorie Green

Dear Professor Burden,
Did you receive my last note? It would be so helpful to see you. When will you signal to me? Events are threatening, but I take refuge in your knowledge of me. My own knowledge is returning, as you must have intended. I am recalling "the great wings beating still" . . . I can hear them. Now the time has come again. "Speech after long silence; it is right . . ."
Perspicaciously,
Dorie

Dear Professor Burden,
Mrs. Rea told me at the mailboxes that you have been ill again. I would ring your bell, but I am so afraid of disturbing you. I met a man in the hallway who said he was bringing you food. If you would only tell me how I could help you now. You could let me. My heart is being hammered into gold.
Abidingly,
Dorie Green

My dear Professor Burden,
It has been difficult for me to breathe, knowing you are ill. I believe
and trust that we are "the yolk and white of the one shell." I am
going to make you a pudding. I will knock on your door at six
o'clock tomorrow night.

Your Leda, D.G.

Thomas sighed, took out a sheet of typewriter paper, which he
tore carefully in half, and began to write.

Dear Miss Green;
You must excuse my not answering your knock last night, but I
was really not fit to receive your kindness. For an old man like
me, I am making tolerable progress, but my condition at the mo-
ment would only make you uncomfortable and be an embarrass-
ment to me. By the way, I am glad you are enjoying the poetry,
although I assure you that the connections you are drawing out of
it in regards to me do not exist.

Thomas pressed his lips together and thought about the face of
Dorie Green. The last time they had spoken together in the
hallway he had noticed an angry rash of some sort on her chin
and along her jaw line. It had been a complete mistake, he decided now, ever to have been friendly to her. He should have
recognized this disturbed, narcissistic type and stayed clear.
Even this letter might be a mistake. Well, perhaps he could
extricate himself. He continued:

Thanks to the splendid ministrations of my former wife, I am
receiving curative food. I am also looking forward to the arrival of
my daughter at the end of next week. With best wishes to you and
many thanks for your thoughtfulness,

Yours,
Thos. Burden

He sealed the note in one of the small, cheap envelopes he used for paying bills and set it on the brim of his straw hat, already laid out with his umbrella on the table. Then he crumpled up all of Dorie Green's notes in distaste, stuffed them into the kitchen garbage—banana peels, tea bags, this morning's egg shell—and carried the bag directly down the hallway to the incinerator chute. He washed his hands and combed his hair. Poor girl, she was really sounding quite mad; certainly she was more than he could be expected to handle right now, in his condition. Thomas looked at his own face in the bathroom mirror: but should he attempt, he wondered, to find out where her parents lived and try to speak to them about her? Her disturbed voice really was alarming. But what if they were as deluded as she? What if they were to implicate and involve him? Horrors. He closed his eyes for a moment and gripped the edge of the wash basin.

Thomas found that he was trembling a little as he gathered up his hat and umbrella and the letter. He shook his head at himself. After all these years of observation, he should have recognized Dorie Green's type—desperately grasping, depressed most of the time, probably, when she wasn't euphoric with her grandiose delusions. He should have known better than to extend himself in response to her.

In the hallway he looked swiftly about and then crossed over to Dorie Green's door and slid the envelope beneath it. There. He put on his hat. He would put forth absolutely no more energy in her direction, and hopefully she would not be able to continue in her obsession with him. On the landing of the stairs, Thomas's body shook involuntarily for a moment, all over, like an animal. Human beings, he thought, could indeed be alarming.

Out into the hazy sunlight he stepped, blinking. His eyes, his whole body felt weak. The air was heavy with moisture, warm, laced through with pollution. Down the block a rented truck was being loaded by some of the shabby students who perennially came and went. Students. He supposed his heart should go out to them, but there were too many these days; he was afraid there wasn't going to be room in the world for all this ambition, or lack of it, all this need—too many students, too many inferior books, too many felled trees. Thomas sniffed at the air and bore down along the sidewalk past the students, tapping the cement with his umbrella.

Once around the block brought him to the limit of his energy. Sarah's neighborhood, though only a dozen blocks away, had been too far for him since this latest flare-up, and he had been noticing that his was apparently too far for her. Food she sent, Otto she sent, but she herself she withheld—not that he would have wanted to see her, oh no. Her ideas, sweet as they might sound, could never be sustained. At least if you held to yourself there was no pretense. What you had to do was prepare yourself for solitary confrontations with nothingness; you couldn't go around asking people to hold your hand.

Toiling up the stairs to his apartment, Thomas cursed himself. More and more, every day, he was becoming a piece of baggage to be heaved and lugged here and there. At his own landing, he cast a glance sodden with mistrust at the door of Miss Dorthea Green; he could feel that he was already bracing himself against future gifts of pudding or more notes torn from a writing tablet of overly bright colored sheets. Even safely inside his own door, he did not feel protected from her extreme and unpredictable want. The Girl Who Needs to Adore had become the Starving, Cannibal Woman. He was a fool to have fed her a book of poetry: now she was looking to him for the whole banquet. How absurd it was that she should have fixed upon such an ornery old piece of leather like himself.

Thomas collapsed into his chair by the table and let his head fall back to the cushion. His mouth was open. He heard his own exhausted breathing and felt his eyes wanting to roll toward unconsciousness. There was something he needed to recall, a thought that had come to him a moment ago in the stairwell, something logical, something he must do—what was it? He breathed heavily and concentrated. Then he heard himself begin to snore and woke up, closing his mouth into a grimace. Food. Yes, he must call Sarah immediately and stop these dinners, that was it—if he could just get up out of this chair. He must cut off her little game before it went too far, before both of them were so terribly hurt again. Sarah might think she knew what she was doing, but she didn't, really. She was a disarming child, playing with the weapons of a woman. It was up to him now to protect both of them from any more falseness. This was something he could do, out of his long habit of severity and self-control, a step he could take, for both of them—all of them. Thomas tried to concentrate on heaving himself out of the chair and crossing the room to the telephone, but he couldn't seem to work himself up to do it. His own mind seemed to be saying to him, *Never mind, never mind.*

In a little while raindrops began mixing with the nodding motions of the tree-of-heaven leaves. It was a gentle rain, coming down and down. Drops fell on the large leaves, collected, slid off toward the alley. Well. It was just an afternoon rain, like hundreds of others—and yet like how many more? He sat watching the rain. How many more rains would he live to see? There was a blot in his mind as he tried to understand how he had gotten to this particular afternoon. He couldn't quite wake up to it. And he was still thinking that he should get himself out of this chair and cross the room to the telephone.

Sarah Burden had loved the telephone. She would hurry to answer it, and always in her voice there would be a lift of anticipation. She would push her hair up from her forehead or the back of her neck. She would laugh at something he could not hear. Friends from long ago would call. "Oh!" she would exclaim. "I'm so glad to hear your voice!" "That was Suzanne," she might say to him as she put down the receiver and came over to his reading chair. In the early years she had made a game of taking the book from his hands, placing it aside, and setting herself confidently in his lap to tell him what Suzanne had said, or Joan, or Margaret, or her brothers Robert and Page. These names came easily to him, all at once, as if a compartment had opened. He remembered how the young Sarah would sit in his lap, making a game of distracting him, taking off his glasses, unbuttoning his shirt. And hadn't he laughed with her? Hadn't he told her that she was a whole glorious lapful? Hadn't he promised her that he would tuck her permanently under his arm and take her with him always? There was a blot when Thomas tried to make a connection between that clear memory of young Sarah on his lap and this bleary, stupefying moment.

With his eyes on the rain, he waited, neither asleep nor awake. Above him and around him, weighing on him as if he were imprisoned inside the earth's gravity instead of resting on its surface, was a load of fatigue and wrong-headedness so dense it seemed impossible anything could burst through it.

After a time the rain stopped, and the sun shone on the wet leaves. He wondered if he had completed a vigil of some sort. He rested his head against the wing of the chair and fell completely asleep this time, waking only as the doorbell rang. Jolted, he answered it like a sleepwalker and almost wordlessly accepted the familiar basket from Otto.

"Shall I sit with you?" asked Otto.

"I think not tonight," he heard himself say. "I'm quite tired."

He ate the meal. How many more? he asked himself. For dessert there was a cup of custard with a sweet, nutmeg-spiced film on top. As he had when he was a child, he ate systematically to the bottom of the cup, to see what he would find there.

Then he carried the dishes to his tiny kitchen, rinsed and left them in the sink, and went directly to the bathroom for a shower. Naked, clean, long-boned, wrinkled, pale, with less flesh on him now than there had been for years, he carried his small pile of clothing to the bedroom and rummaged for a pair of clean pajamas. He turned off the bedroom air conditioner and opened the window next to it.

This was the hour, not yet dark, during which the youngest children were put to bed. He remembered how as a child he had protested one night at being alone in his bed when it was still so light and active outside. Unable to sleep, he had gone to his window and seen his parents below in the garden, by the arched trellis, close to each other, arms curved outward: his mother and father had been kissing. Tommy had been four or five years old. *Wait for me,* he had wanted to shout, perhaps had shouted. He had wanted to fly straight from the sill of his window to the spot in the garden where the kissing was going on without him. Instead, he had crept guiltily down the stairs and out the kitchen door, barefoot, in his nightshirt. That was all he could remember. He knew he had gone outside, but he didn't know what had happened next, whether they had been angry, who had taken him back to bed. And he had never been able to understand why the kissing had one day stopped.

Thomas tightened the bottom sheet on his still unmade bed and eased himself down onto it. Without the air conditioner on, he would hear everything—the gathering birds, a car door slamming, even voices and steps of passers-by. He heard a muffled radio voice from another apartment. The evening was so permeable to sound that all partitions seemed flimsy. Somewhere he had read of city dwellers in India dragging their bedding out into the courtyard during warm weather and sleeping all together under the sky. Here, they could do the same, he supposed, out onto the poor strip of yard between apartment houses, or the back fire escapes, or even the jumbled alley. He snorted to himself: there they would be—the whole cast of characters, smacking their lips, settling down, sighing, snoring, their individual follies gradually subsumed by sleep. They'd have to trust in each other; it would be impossible for them to close their eyes otherwise.

A surge of alarm went through him as he remembered the

note he had written to Dorie Green and as he considered how her troubled mind might be construing his words. His hands swept out across a bedsheet too smooth to grasp. He reminded himself that he didn't trust her, and he didn't much like her. Was it his fault that Miss Dorie Green was off in the head? He assured himself that he was alone, that his locked door and the walls of his apartment had secured this space for him. There were partitions, mercifully. Thank god her life was not his. He was glad he had not been born a woman. Busily, busily, all these thoughts were sliding across his mind, but mercifully did not seem to be taking hold. He wanted to be without them.

What was more interesting, more pleasing was to lie bathed and bedded like a child, this time comforted by the surrounding sounds of ordinary life. He thought he could probably sleep now. He lay lightly, above the torpor of the afternoon. Nothing was taking hold. He was not minding anything. He wasn't exactly sleeping, for he still heard everything—evening sounds turning into night sounds, laughter, and then more laughter. Men and women were laughing. He seemed to hear Sarah's voice among the others. It was almost as if they were all standing in the next room, laughing. He tried to open his eyes but could not, because now he was sleeping, he knew he was sleeping. *Wait for me,* he could not rise to speak. The night was being taken over by men's voices and women's voices, laughing and laughing. The doors gave way, all the walls gave way, and a flood of laughter was coming in.

II

The time is coming, said Dorie Green's notes. *Birds speak of how I am waiting. My fire is making me valuable and irresistible, you will not believe it.* Under the door at nearly predictable hours came these fragments of language, poetic, manic, encroaching. Thomas's hands would shake as he opened the colored envelopes to

"Professor Burden." The script was cramped, oddly slanted, all ups and downs with no loops, no flow between the letters. Even to let his eyes travel over the uneasy strands of marks without attempting comprehension made him uncomfortable, which was absurd, he thought, to allow himself to be threatened by a poor girl who was only clutching out at life, and at him, through words. He had resolved not to respond to the notes, and after a few more days he decided that it would be better if he did not even open them. Each one he meticulously threw away, not in the open basket beside his desk, but deep inside the bag of kitchen garbage, which he dropped into the incinerator chute each afternoon before his walk.

She was too much for him. He would do nothing. The fitfulness of his own existence was all he could manage. Anyway, what would happen would happen. Patience. About patience Miss Dorthea Green knew nothing yet. He had nearly half a century more of disappointment than she to acquire his own miserable store of patience.

A few days before Martha was to come for her visit, Sarah called to invite Thomas out to dinner with them to celebrate Martha's first night home, but he replied that a restaurant would really be too much for him to handle. "I'm much better, but I still need to keep things simple," he said. Then Sarah told him that she and Otto were going out of town overnight and that she was glad he was so much improved because now he would probably enjoy puttering about with his own dinners. "Probably," he said, but it was odd the effect her words had on him. Stopping the baskets himself would have been one thing, an honest, straightforward attempt on his part to set things straight; the baskets stopping on account of Sarah was another matter. Thomas sealed his lips together and thought about his present condition and about old pains.

But after a day or two it became a relief not to have to answer the door for the basket. His meals were indeed simple. The weather turned beastly hot and humid, and he crept out only when absolutely necessary, to stretch his legs and buy a few provisions. Other than this, he kept completely to himself. He almost took pleasure in the becalmed nothingness of his days and in the way his clothes hung on his nearly ascetic body. *Bare bones,* he would say, half aloud. *Bare bones.* Sometimes as he chewed on his bread or sipped his weak tea, he imagined himself a prisoner who has reached a level of sublimity impossible for those on the outside who squander freedom daily.

Then one afternoon the telephone rang, just as he had been in the midst of a reverie in which he was giving away most of his possessions to Martha and moving into a single room, and it was Martha herself, on her second day home, saying that she was on her way over and he was supposed to put a smile on his face and open the door for her. Her voice, he thought, sounded almost pert.

Immediately after embracing him, Martha demanded to know why there was a trail of what looked like bread crumbs in his hallway.

"Bread crumbs?" Thomas felt stupid, not sublime, standing there in the middle of his living room not at all understanding what his daughter was talking about. How elderly and unsteady he must appear! Reunions were so often awkward and of course never how you imagined them.

Martha took his hand and drew him to the door. "It's very odd," she said.

At the threshold Thomas looked down upon a scattering of pale crumbs that led along the carpeting in an uneven line to the apartment opposite. He wanted to blink and make the trail vanish. His heart began to pound, and he stepped back into his room. "This is something new," he said.

"What is it about?" asked Martha. "Who lives over there?"

Thomas motioned her to come in and close the door. She was quick in her movements, lean, like him—though not as lean at the moment as she usually was. Her straight, brown, graying hair was parted on the side and flipped casually over one eyebrow, and her tailored trousers and shirt hung in various pleats and folds from her angular body.

Let me get a look at you, he wanted to say, but she was so graceful that he felt more than ever unsteady himself. He turned toward his chair and lowered himself into it.

"Now then, what's going on?" asked Martha as she swung up the camera case she had left by the door and brought herself and her equipment to the straight-backed chair by the library table. Since her college years he had scarcely ever seen her without a many pocketed bag of some sort filled with cameras and lenses and sometimes even a tape recorder. He watched her let the bag slide to the floor beside the chair, half-expecting her to pull out the camera immediately and catch him there in his day-old summer shirt, his sinewed neck, his unsteadiness.

"So what is that mess in the hallway all about?" she asked as she pulled her chair closer to his. She reached out and tapped his knee. "You don't look well. There's perspiration on your forehead. Do you know what is going on?"

He opened his mouth, but there were no words ready to be spoken. He felt like sinking away. *Be still,* he wanted to say, *let's both be still, please.* As a child she had always moved too much for him, spoken too much, asked for too much, slept too erratically. From the first he had felt inadequate: he had known he would. Hadn't he said just that to Sarah? Hadn't he told her there wouldn't be enough of him for a child? And Sarah had probably laughed then, too, in that way of hers.

"Who lives across the hall?" demanded Martha. "That trail of crumbs looks like something out of a story."

"It's stranger than most," he said to her, trying to clear his throat, "not what one would choose."

"What does it mean?"

"It means I'm an old fool."

"But who lives there?"

"A young woman who thinks I'm someone I'm not, who thinks I understand her and everything else." He shook his head and grimaced, in derision of himself.

"I don't understand," said Martha.

"Nor do I. What little I thought I may have known has broken down completely. I'm an old fool."

Without a word Martha got up and disappeared behind him. He could hear her opening the refrigerator, banging ice cube trays, running water. She returned with two glasses of plain water. "Here's to you," she said. "You've been calling yourself an old fool for as long as I can remember."

"Have I really?" He took a tentative drink of water. Ice cubes were perhaps not the best thing at the moment, he thought.

"Yes. Don't you get tired of it?"

"Apparently not."

"What do the bread crumbs have to do with it?"

"I would prefer not to use my imagination."

"Who is she?"

"A librarian. Somewhere around thirty. I spoke some few words to her, loaned her a book—who knows? She has fixed on me. She must be desperate indeed." He rested his head on the back of his chair and looked at his daughter from beneath half-lowered lids. Even now, only moments after her return, he felt that he was falling away from their reunion, sinking, not rising toward it. *Be still, don't make me talk.*

"But what has happened? Something must have happened."

There must be something terribly wrong with him, he thought, that he was not better at this business of living. How did people ever manage to please each other?

"Be still a minute," he heard himself say. "May I please just have the pleasure of looking at you for a minute?"

Now it was her turn to make a gesture of self-deprecation. "You know well enough what I look like—I look like you."

"Is that what you think?"

"That's what everyone says." Martha tossed off these words as she set down her glass and opened her camera case.

"Do you think you look like me?" he asked.

"Somewhat. I haven't thought about it for a while." She changed lenses, made a series of small adjustments, and held the camera to her eye, pointed at him.

"I don't believe the light is good enough in here," he said.

"It's fine. This film is very fast."

"I don't know anything about it," he said self-consciously, waiting for the click. He endured the moment. He felt himself forever held within this room, imprinted with slatted afternoon light. He did not see how such imperfect people could ever help or please each other.

"What has this librarian said to you?" Martha spoke as she advanced the film and walked out into the room to capture him from another angle. He glanced over at her, slouched and concentrating, and could almost see what she saw: himself in limpness, the chair, the broad oak table with stacks of magazines and books on its top and its low shelf, the old-fashioned table lamp, its double bulbs shaded in fluted glass, the Venetian blinds, the tree of heaven. She shot him twice and then returned to her chair. "Well?" she asked.

"I'd show you her little letters, but I've destroyed them all. She slides them under my door. Lately I haven't even had the stomach to open them."

"You're frightened," said Martha.

"It's too much for an old man. I believe she's quite troubled. Mentally, I mean. It's hard for me to judge."

"Does she telephone?"

"No, I've at least had the wits to tell very few people my unlisted number."

"Does she knock?"

"I may have heard a knock once or twice, but I usually have that noisy air conditioner on. I go out only when she's at work."

"What about weekends?"

"I'm extremely careful. And of course I haven't been feeling well all month. I only venture out briefly. And it has been so humid. The air has been too heavy."

"Does Mother know about this?"

"No, I would have been embarrassed to trouble her with it."

"This is no way to live!" cried out Martha suddenly. "This is crazy, Dad, really crazy." She left him again for the kitchen and in a moment she was striding across the living room with broom and dust pan and paper bag. She flung open the door and began to sweep. He opened his mouth to protest—it was Saturday; there was no telling whether his neighbor was home or not— but then he clamped his lips together in resignation to fate. What did it matter any longer, one absurdity more or less? He heard her sweeping. He closed his eyes. Martha was right: this was no way to live.

When Martha had finished with her job, safely, and closed the door and come back to sit before him, she seemed angry and impatient, the way she used to be as a child when she would stamp her foot at him and tell him something was unfair. Her sense of justice had been, he thought, unusually strong for a young child and her outcries vociferous. For a long time, she hadn't had an ounce of diplomacy in her. Thomas had found her somewhat less abrasive and exhausting after she left college and acquired a smoother style, her outrages tempered in part by disenchantment. Today, however, she reminded him of the self-righteous child Martha. Beneath his set expression, he watched her with a faint curiosity, just to see what she would do next. And he wondered if a younger Thomas would emerge to meet her.

"You shouldn't let yourself get into these states, Dad. I'm sick of them. Why do you let these things happen?"

He laughed outright at her. "Things happen, my dear. At least I can tell you that much from my scant store of wisdom. I did not invent this poor young woman. I'm afraid she is the one who is inventing me."

"*Afraid!*" exclaimed Martha. "That's the word for it—you're afraid of everything. You're afraid of living."

"Aren't those rather harsh words to be using on your old father?"

"Yes," she said, "they are." She sat looking at him, silently, as he had been wanting her to do. She wasn't even fiddling with her camera case, either, just looking.

"Listen, Dad," she said after a time and in a gentler voice, "I want you to come with us to the lake tomorrow."

He cleared his throat noisily. "I don't think I can do that."

"You have to. Would you do it for me?"

"You three would have a far better time without me." He heard himself speaking, but what he was seeing was Martha as a child asleep in his arms, when she would fall asleep somewhere and need to be carried home, and he would carry the warm weight of her, blessedly quiet and undemanding except for the one basic need of being carried from one place to another, gently, with care that she should not wake unnecessarily.

"We three without you would probably be thinking about you," said Martha.

"Surely you could find better things to think about."

"No doubt." Martha was still looking at him steadily, almost impertinently.

Now is the time I should die, he was thinking. He returned the gaze of his unmarried daughter and said to her, "If I were to die, it would make things easier for you. You could live your life."

"I am living my life," said Martha. She spread out her hands on either side of her face in a clownish gesture. "See? It's the real me." And then she added, "In case you hadn't noticed."

"You mustn't feel responsible for me. You and Sarah would be much better off if you didn't feel responsible. Otto, too." Thomas widened his eyes in challenge upon his daughter. He was surprised at himself, at the way he was talking along almost glibly, the words so easy and terrible.

"It's not as easy as that," said Martha.

"I don't have much steam left," he said. "And I'm not making that up, my dear. There just isn't much of me left. I have no desires anymore."

"I don't believe you."

"Just wait. You'll have your turn. Someday you'll see."

"I don't think you have any right to talk like this. It isn't fair! Do you have any idea the effect it has?"

"Everything is beyond me now," he said. "Fate is taking over."

"What nonsense!" Martha began putting her camera away with angry gestures. Everything seemed at the same time banal and extremely terrible—he and Martha facing each other in discomfort, Sarah in that house of hers, blithely making plans, Otto off gathering in money and pretending he knew what order was, and beyond Thomas's closed door, across the hallway, behind another door that desperate young woman, who this very moment might be pressing up against a crack in her door, watching his, who might have watched Martha enter or watched her sweep, who might have found a way to listen to this conversation, to watch his face, even here. Anything was possible. A lid of weakness lowered over him.

"I've been ill," he whispered. "You can't know what it's like when you are disgusting to yourself."

He heard Martha get up and cross over to the kitchen. For a moment it seemed that she might have decided to stay and cook a little supper for both of them, and the thought was not displeasing. He felt too weak to move. But she came back quickly, and he opened his eyes to see her swinging her camera bag to her shoulder. She did not sit down again.

"I'm going to have dinner with my old friend Mary Lou tonight," she said. "But tomorrow I will come and pick you up for the lake. I think you'll be glad you came. It's only for a few days, Dad. You can do that."

"I have no clean clothes," he said. "It has been too hot for the laundry room."

"No problem," said Martha breezily. "There's a washer at the cottage."

"Martha, I can't go. I can't do this to you."

"Do what!" She actually stamped her foot, and Thomas was almost startled into laughing, with the memories that were rising up in him like a pungent dust from another time.

"It's absurd, my dear—don't you see?" He paused. "Your mother . . . she's married . . . to this other guy." He was appalled to hear his own voice breaking.

"Do you think I don't know that, do you think I haven't been living with that, too?" Martha was speaking fiercely. She stood with hands clenched, not so much now the smooth, well-traveled, hard-working young woman. It seemed to Thomas that they had never spoken quite like this to each other. In the old days he might even have said to her at such a time that she should go to her room and calm herself, that he had work to do, a deadline to meet, that he didn't need to listen to any more nonsense and he would talk to her when she had gotten control of herself.

All of a sudden, now, without his saying anything, she did get control of herself; her posture changed, and one hand flipped back her hair and came down to rest on a hip. A smile appeared on her face. "I have something to tell you, Dad, but I'm not going to say it here or now. I want to pick you up tomorrow morning at eight-thirty and take you to the lake. Otto and Sarah will go in their car. Will you please come?"

He said nothing.

"You'll come," she said, and she turned and opened that dangerous door and left him in his apartment.

For dinner Thomas made himself a bowl of instant farina. Milk rushed in to fill the craters left by his scooping spoon. This drama lasted until all there was left to eat was a thin gruel.

Thomas stared at the bowl and at his hands. Was there anything left of him, he wondered, besides ill temper? Slowly he spooned up the sweet gruel. He had always considered himself a civilized man, had always thought himself lucky at least to be in the line of Western civilization, but it was odd how that word sounded to him now: *civilization*. He didn't think he knew what anything meant anymore.

About eight o'clock that night he looked up from his reading—a memoir of China that wasn't half bad—to see a peach-colored envelope being slid under his door. As he stared at the envelope, he wondered about old age in China, whether there might be more to it, in China. There had been no knock of which he was aware, but of course the air conditioner made one feel numb to sound after a time. At about nine he finally got up and went over to pick up the envelope. He took it back to his chair and stared at it for a long time. Finally he broke into it.

Dear Professor Burden,
I am tending my fire, and now your messages are reaching me easily, as you intended. They are very beautiful. I am overwhelmed that you are taking such care with me. No one has ever taken such care. Now you must let me help you. I was nothing before you flew down to me. Feathered glory! You must let me help you. I am the only one who knows you are being held against your will. I think I have known you since time began.

Faithfully,
D.G.

P.S. It would be so very helpful if you could be more specific in your instructions. I need a map so I can be ready when the time comes.

Thomas's hand holding the letter shook as if palsied. He crumpled the paper and made a firm fist, to stop the shaking. What had he done? Almost nothing. Yet in his silence her fabrications had gone on and on. What a terrible thing this was, to be the object of someone's delusion. She had no right ... she had gone too far. He crumpled the paper again, this time angrily, and made himself stand and walk to the kitchen. He cleared his cereal bowl and spoon from the old sink, set the crumpled paper on an iron stain near the drain, and took up the box of matches from the stove and lit one and brought it down to touch the crinkled ball. Slowly the beginnings of fire made their way inward, and then all of a sudden the entire ball was aflame. Afterwards, the ashes retained some of the shape of the crinkles. With a cooking spoon he brought everything down to a flat heap, and then he turned on the faucet and flushed the heap away. A dark smudge remained, on top of the orange-brown iron stain. Thomas got out the cleansing powder and began to scrub. He scrubbed and rinsed and scrubbed until the gray mark had disappeared. He didn't bother about the rest of the sink.

When Martha came for him in the morning, the second of July, he was completely ready to walk out the door: seersucker suit, straw hat, old leather suitcase, even two bananas, which, he said to her quite cheerfully, would certainly be far beyond their prime if he left them behind. He had turned off the lights, unplugged the air conditioner and the radio. He had even paid two bills, now neatly in his breast pocket. He had gotten himself in hand: he was presentable; he was presenting himself. In such a world what was left for him but to put on his clothes and see what would happen next? He pretended to Martha that there had never been any question about his coming. She had wanted him to come: so, here he was.

He handed her the bananas with a slight bow.

"Many thanks," she said, laughing. "We'll eat them in the car. Mother packed a few other edibles, too."

"Yes, she would, wouldn't she? Sarah's care packages."

"You're looking better today, Dad. You must have had a good sleep."

"Yes, quite a good sleep," he said loudly as they stepped out into the hallway. He jangled his keys and locked up with a flourish. He cast not even a glance at the door across the hall. He was leaving: let Miss Dorie Green take a good look if she wanted to. Martha was carrying his suitcase. "You go ahead of me," he said. "I'll need some time on the stairs."

Dirtied Sunday light from above shone down into the well of stairs. Martha's long body ahead of him was taking the stairs easily, head slightly bent, and as she rounded a landing he saw how her hair fell over her right eye and cheek, how her hand on the next bannister, her smooth arm, her throat were a warm summer color, not bad looking even in this awful light, how her body in spite of its angularity was a woman's body, inside those loose clothes: yes, a woman's body, such as he had always thought he should be grateful not to have to live inside. In full view they descended, first the daughter and then the father, and above them perhaps was a viewer, an eye in a crack, a female eye. An old feeling of advantage and power made a tiny upward motion in Thomas. He was the man here. At least he was not one of the women. If there was fate for men, women were fated twice over, a hundred times over by nature: they were Fate personified. Poor creatures. At least he had escaped that much. Down he went, in full view.

Martha drove a small, plain car, and the interior of it was never particularly neat. It seemed to Thomas that he always had to remove something from a seat before he could sit down—a piece of camera equipment or a book or a discarded plastic food box or a catalogue of some sort. She always had various sweaters and shoes and hats and magazines strewn on the back seat and window ledge, always several partly crushed boxes of tissue. Today there was a half-empty box of soda crackers on the front passenger seat.

"I'll take those," said Martha, and she deftly shoved them under the driver's seat. The bananas she had already tossed into a basket in the back seat. Thomas's suitcase had gone into the trunk so quickly he had a moment just as they were pulling away of wondering whether she had put it in at all; he craned around to see an empty curb, a mottled lawn, a facade he scarcely ever regarded anymore, of itself. He had almost forgotten that the windows on the first floor of the apartment building were arched, that twisted columns flanked the door, and that some care had been taken, long ago, to vary the patterning of the brick. It was a building of nostalgia for a homeland, or several homelands, or the idea of a homeland. Behind the departing car trees flew up to block his view. Above the branches were the upper stories, his own disappearing front window, a tile roof against the blue sky.

Martha turned at the corner, his street was gone, and Thomas faced around again. The sun was in his lap. He massaged his long, liver-spotted hands in the warmth. "It's not half bad out today," he said. "Not so humid. I have a lot of trouble in that humidity."

"Most people do," said Martha. She had put on a pair of large sunglasses and was settling into the business of driving. "Comfortable, Dad? The seat belt is up there to your right."

"I don't abide by them, thank you," said Thomas.

"That's ridiculous," said Martha. "Everyone wears seat belts these days."

"I won't, thank you. They seem to irritate my condition."

"What condition?"

He found himself giving out a laugh. "Well, whatever condition is making its show at any particular time."

"And today?"

"Actually, today I have less static than I've had for a while. I'm quite grateful to have my digestion straightened out somewhat. And the stiffness in my neck is nearly gone—did I tell you about that? It was very troublesome."

"Tell me about it while you put on your seat belt."

He looked at her in surprise, and she glanced at him full-face for an instant—huge dark glasses, painted mouth, angular, determined jaw. "I mean it," she said. "It makes me nervous when people flirt around with safety."

"You don't sound like yourself. I've never heard you insist on seat belts before."

"Think of Mother," said Martha. "Without the belt she would have been dead, they said. As it was, it was bad enough."

"To have lost your mother would have been a loss indeed. Dead wood like me is quite another matter."

"If you knew how you sounded, you wouldn't talk that way," said Martha. She began to slow the car toward the curb at a bus stop. "Put it on."

He laughed and threw up his hands. "I submit to the lady at the wheel." But irritation did race through him as he struggled with a mechanism that he supposed was easy to most people but himself. "I don't like too many contrivances," he said. "It's a good thing I left the newspaper business before computers came in—I never could have tolerated them." He was trying hard to be good-natured and conversational, helped along all this while by a small sense of triumph, a mingling of tiny victories: of having managed to put together this morning a semblance of a civilized man; of having gotten away safely from the sphere of Miss Dorie Green; of remembering one bracing bit of fact—that he was a man after all, by god, not one of the women.

"They could make these belts a good deal less cumbersome," he said.

"I think they've tried to," said Martha. She took the buckle end from his hands and plugged it into a central slot. "There. Can you breathe?" Did he hear mockery in her voice?

"Quite well. Now don't go crashing us up just to prove your point about these awful belts."

"How could I do that when I had you for a driving teacher?"

"That's right," he said. "That was something we did, wasn't it?"

"Yes, that was something we did. You seemed to like it."

"We would go out in the evenings after dinner, as I recall."

"Usually. And you were unusually patient. I never understood why you were so patient in that instance and so impatient generally."

"Oh, really?" He wasn't about to concede anything, but it was true he had enjoyed those self-contained after dinner hours in the car with Martha. They had been going nowhere, but with a purpose, burning cheap gas, leaving the house behind them. Often there had been sunsets. Sarah had shown her fright of the whole process, and knowing her fear had sometimes incited Thomas to stay out even later on the road, with their only child.

"Yes, really," said Martha. "You were a pretty good teacher."

"You've turned out to be a much better driver than your mother. With her, I tried, but she has her ways."

Martha made no reply. They had reached the interchange onto the freeway, and now the trip was really beginning. Thomas didn't think he had been outside of town in well over a year. He had no car himself now. He didn't really have the money to keep one up and, besides, he had started to feel too irritable, too shaky while driving. "I'm a hazard," he had told one of the few friends he had left from the newspaper. "I'm a hazard and a liability in almost any way you can name."

They turned north, and the sun came in on Thomas's right cheek and shoulder. He tilted his straw hat to one side, as a shield. They were still in the region of clean industry, suburban office buildings, used car lots. The light was terribly bright, worse as it glanced off metal. Thomas closed his eyes. He was getting away, he was escaping. If he were never to return, that would fix Miss Dorie Green, wouldn't it? That would show her he couldn't be appropriated.

In this sun he was drowsy. And there was something pleasantly risky about closing his eyes and putting himself in the hands of a daughter he had set on the road so long ago; it might be better than being at the wheel himself. If at this moment they were to crash and death were to come toward him from the hands of his own child, it might be the right death for him, economical and symmetrical: from him she came, from her he went. For an instant he opened his eyes upon a flat white corporate headquarters with an artificial moat of water glinting along its expensive length, and then quickly closed them again. It could happen now, this death; he didn't think he cared. He was almost comforted to be falling drowsily toward the interior of the motion of their journey, indifferent, with Martha up there somewhere at the wheel. Perhaps he had never before felt so truly grateful or comforted to have a child.

He woke to realize that the car had stopped at a gas station, and Martha was preparing to get out. She stuffed the box of soda crackers back under the seat.

"Bathroom?" she asked, still chewing on a cracker. "You've been sleeping for a long time."

"Yes, all right."

"Then we could find some place for our picnic."

"All right," he said. "We'll see what Sarah has for us this time."

They found a wooded wayside on the rise of a hill, with two outhouses, some scattered tables, and a hand pump beneath a shelter. Thomas steadied himself by the side of the car and then headed straight for the pump. A breeze, carrying traces of coolness and the scent of pines, blew over the hill. Thomas had pumped water to the surface and out the two openings, an upper drinking fountain and a lower spout, before he realized he had left the picnic things for Martha to carry.

"Sorry," he called out.

"No trouble." Martha set down the basket and came over for the drink he was offering. He tried to pump so that the jet remained as steady as possible. She leaned forward elaborately to avoid the lower spatters and held the swoop of her hair back with one hand.

"Iron flavored," she pronounced. "Have you had some? Here, I'll pump for you."

He drank and then drank again. Everything about the place was reminiscent to him, but especially the pump. The place was here for travelers, countless travelers; it was very possible that he had been here before, probably with Sarah, years and years ago.

"Dad," said Martha when he had straightened up, "I want to tell you something right now. I'm pregnant. In seven months, a little less, I'm going to have this baby." Thomas allowed his eyes to follow the downward direction of her glance and the quick, intimate, rounded gesture of her hands.

Embarrassed, he rested his hand on the cold pump casing. "How can that be?" he asked.

Martha was studying him, something like a smile in her features. "Do you want me to tell you exactly?"

"You're not married. You can't be thinking of raising a child."

"I'm not just thinking about it any longer. Now I'm going to do it."

"You *planned* it?"

"Yes, I planned it."

Another car was just then pulling into the wayside. "I think I should sit down," said Thomas. He took up the basket and walked slowly toward one of the tables. He sat down with his back to the road and the other people. The woods were deep beyond the mowed area of the wayside. He watched a squirrel jump from one tree to another, leaping the gap and riding out the bobbing of the branch with scarcely a pause, followed right away by another squirrel. Thomas thought that he might indeed have been here before, but he couldn't tell for sure. Even Martha's words seemed to have been said before, if not in this place, then in a place like this. He turned for another look at the pump.

"Well?" said Martha. She had sat down opposite him and was beginning to take wrapped sandwiches from the basket.

"I'm very surprised, and then again I'm not surprised at all. Do you think I've lived too long to be surprised any longer?"

"It's the baby we're talking about," said Martha.

"This might be too much for me," said Thomas.

Martha unwrapped a sandwich, lifted a corner of the bread for a look inside, and then handed it over to Thomas. Her own she unwrapped and bit into immediately. "How much shall I tell you?" she asked.

Thomas regarded the layers of bread, meat, and cheese before him. Sarah had given him no mayonnaise and no lettuce; she knew his preference. In fact, knowing his likes and dislikes had always been one of her talents. She had seemed to enjoy trying to please him, and he had assumed this was in her nature, to enjoy pleasing him. He took a bite of the sandwich she had made for him.

"Do your mother and Otto know about this?"

"Yes, I've told them. They say they are willing to support my decision—the standard response. I suppose it's going to take all of you a while to understand this."

"We'll all be dead before the job is half over," said Thomas. "What kind of family is that for a child?" He noticed that Martha was eating her sandwich rather too quickly. He slowed down his own chewing and thought with a small flickering of pleasure about the spareness of himself, the skin covering his bones, eyes looking out without expectation. Then something about the way Martha was licking her fingers and searching the basket for more food reminded him of the disorderly interior of her car.

"How can you be thinking of having a child when you have a car that looks like yours does inside?"

With her hand still inside the tipped basket, Martha stopped and scrutinized his face. He looked right back at her. Somewhere overhead one of the squirrels chittered a repeated message.

"Do you want to know something, Dad? I'll tell you. I'm not afraid of you any longer. And I used to be very much afraid. Did you know that? I think what I was afraid of was your scorn. Now ... well, now I don't have any more time to be afraid of your scorn."

Thomas put the rest of his sandwich back into the plastic bag, with no plans for taking it out again. He wiped his fingers on his napkin. "I wouldn't hazard a guess as to what all of this means," he said. "You've always been a stubborn child. If any young man had come to me saying he wanted to marry you, I would have said just that: she's stubborn, you'll be getting a handful." He blinked his eyes at her and felt the weakness and wateriness of his vision. "But then no young man ever came, did he? Your young man never came."

"I can't believe I'm hearing what I'm hearing," said Martha. "This is incredible." She made a sweeping motion across the air. "Erase everything and start over. I say to you, Dad, I'm pregnant. I'm going to give birth to your grandchild. Now, what do you say?"

He blinked at her. "I say what I have been saying, Who's going to take care of this child?"

"I am."

"How can you begin to think that will be enough? It's hard enough with two people. Who's the father? He should be spoken to."

"He has been a friend for a long time, but we don't think we'll marry. He travels all the time. He'll be in and out."

"This is absurd."

"Possibly," said Martha. She had lifted out a container of strawberries and was offering it to him with both hands. The sun came down between the trees in just that spot, and in it the strawberries looked unbelievably red, glistening, studded with indigestible seeds.

"I think not, thank you," said Thomas. "I probably shouldn't. Perhaps I'll have one of my bananas later." He couldn't understand why Sarah would have packed strawberries for him.

"Of course," said Martha. "I forgot."

As Thomas watched her eat, he rested the side of his neck in his cupped hand. Then with his fingertips he began to massage the place on his upper back where there was still a trace of that painful crick.

"What were you saying before about your neck?" asked Martha. "Is that where you were having trouble?"

He told her what it had felt like, a knot of misery, and worse when coupled with his disgusting colitis. He told her what a wretched month he had had and how the heavy heat had made everything difficult. Growing old was hell, he said to her, and part of the hell was that you had no strength left to protect yourself against anything. Take that girl back at his apartment building: now what was he supposed to do to free himself from that? Move out? Why, he had been there for nearly twenty years.

Maybe the girl herself would move out, Martha was saying as she put away the remainder of the strawberries. Maybe she would have moved out by the time he returned.

"Maybe for you she will disappear off the face of the earth." Martha slid out from the picnic bench and stood at the end of the table. "Why don't you just say to yourself, As far as I am concerned, this girl will disappear. And then see what happens."

Thomas looked up at her. "Just like that?"

"Yes, just like that."

Thomas was almost ashamed of how much relief her words were giving him. Martha looked tall standing there beside him, powerful. "What is this, some sort of voodoo?" he asked.

"No, nothing like that."

"I'm trying to remember exactly how old you are," he said.

"I'll be thirty-nine next February. And you've always had to ask—do you know that?"

"Thirty-nine," he repeated. "And you say you used to be afraid of me?"

"Yes, I was afraid of your criticism. I was afraid of what you might say."

"I'm sorry," he said, shielding his eyes to get a better look at her against the light and the trees. "I'm very sorry if I did that to you. I don't think those were my intentions."

Martha had slipped one arm through the basket handle and was offering her other hand to him. "And I never meant to be such a difficult child." She wiggled her fingers at him. "Let's go, Dad. If we step on it, we can get there in time for a swim before dinner."

"Swimming! There aren't any places left on this earth that are clean enough for swimming."

"Really? Are you sure?"

He pushed himself up from the table and took her arm. She did appear to be mocking him. "I told you I was an old fool," he said. Walking beside her, he marveled at what a big girl she was, how steady on her feet. Today she seemed even taller than he. "How tall are you, anyway?" he asked.

"Five-foot-ten. Same as for the last twenty years."

"You look taller than that—you look taller than I." He straightened his posture and looked down the fronts of both their bodies. "How much do you weigh?" he asked.

Martha laughed. "More than usual and going up."

"You might be heavier than I am," he said. "This hasn't been much of a summer for eating, for me."

"Are you eating enough?" She unlocked the car door for him, and as he eased himself down onto the seat, he felt the easily foldable shape of himself. "I don't need much. Next to nothing," he said. She closed the door just at the end of his words. He was surprised at all they had been saying to each other. He had been on the verge of saying something more—he wasn't sure exactly what—something about the particular difficulty of this summer, the disappointment of it, after the spring. He thought what it might be like to unburden himself completely to her about the way he really lived. It was surprising him, how many words were coming to him.

"I remember when you were a baby," he said after they were in motion again. "I remember that." Then suddenly he slapped his hand down on the flat plastic between their seats. "Martha, I'm too old to be a new grandfather! If this was going to happen, it should have happened years ago. And you should be married. I can't imagine how you must be seeing things."

"I told you I've been thinking about it a long time. I've thought about it from all sorts of angles."

"But those are daydreams. Raising a child is hard enough with *two* parents."

"There's a group of people I'm thinking of living with, starting this fall. We've been looking at houses."

"Oh, my dear," he said, "You *are* your mother's child. How has she done it? And to think of the education I gave you."

"Thank you. I have appreciated it."

Thomas shook his head. He looked at her sidelong, at her whole body, and then took a deep, sighing breath.

They had been on a two-lane highway for some time and now were approaching a T-shaped crossroads in a town so small Thomas could only think how glad he was not to have to live in it. He knew all there was to know about being wretched in small towns. Straight ahead was a wooden grocery store with a washtub of petunias stuck out on the cement steps. "I'm glad I don't live here," said Thomas.

"But you grew up in a small town. If you did it once, you could do it again. You could do it if you had to."

"Then I'm glad I don't have to."

After a time his mind came around to what she had been saying, about a house. Who were these people she might live with, he wanted to know. What sort of outfit was it to be?

There was a cellist, Martha answered, and an archivist, and another photographer, with whom she could share equipment and a darkroom. And two other children.

Men, too? Thomas hazarded to ask.

One man and one little boy, his son, but no one was married, she said.

How long did she think something like that could last, he wanted to know. What could be more unstable than a household like that?

They would just have to see, said Martha.

"I couldn't do it," said Thomas.

"No one is asking you to."

He felt obscurely hurt. He tipped his hat down again, crossed his arms over his chest, and began to feign sleep. Sidelong, from underneath the hat, he stole another look at her arms, her breasts, her middle. Pregnant. She had really done it to herself this time, in that headstrong way of hers. Well, let her stew in it; let her stew in life. He was damn glad it wasn't he with all that ahead.

He was reminded what a victory, of sorts, it was that after all the troubles he had had of late he had put himself together today, a semblance of an urbane man, with a straw hat and decent shoes, a good suitcase, a respectable retirement ... and a daughter who wanted to take him places ... and a wife from the past who still, in a way, embraced him.

He nodded off, and when he woke he was sweating. He took off his hat and folded and refolded his handkerchief as he mopped his head and neck. Around a bend appeared a lake, a cluster of cabins, a bait and tackle shop, a couple of northwoods taverns. Martha pulled into a drive-in snack shop.

"Bathroom? Ice cream?" she asked, already getting out.

"I don't care to get out, but I'll take a small vanilla, thank you." Then he had to call after her, "Have the ice cream put in a cup. With a spoon. Please."

Martha finished a large cone while he was still taking small mouthfuls on the plastic spoon. They didn't speak much. She got out of the car again and went to the ladies' room. When she came back, she was carrying a cup of water for each of them. She leaned in and handed his to him and then sat down. She reached under the seat and brought up a handful of crackers, which she ate methodically, taking small sips of the water. Then she crumpled up the cup, dropped it beside the brake lever, brushed off her hands and her lap and started the motor. She flipped back her hair and blew upwards over her face. Thomas was still working away at his ice cream.

"You've really bitten off a chunk now," he said to her. "You've got more ahead of you than you know."

III

"That's sweet fern," said Sarah, pointing with her cane. "These dark glossy leaves are wintergreen." Further along the path she nudged a worm of blackish excrement with the toe of her canvas shoe. "Raccoon scat," she said. "And look over there—beavers' work. Stop here, Thomas, this is the pine hit by lightning. Poor tree, I don't think it can survive. Look at that terrible wound."

Thomas looked up dutifully at the long, spiraled gash, which the tree might still be trying to fill with more of itself.

"It happened last September," said Sarah. "When the lightning hit, everything sounded dead for a second afterwards. Otto and I couldn't tell how close it had touched down."

Thomas considered the stricken tree, which was inclining toward the lake. "When it falls, it will probably fall into the water," he said.

"Yes, unless Otto gets someone in here first to take it down. He likes to hire people to come in and clean out the woods. Chain saws. Terrible things, but they do get the job done. Sometimes Otto works with the men, but I go to town when I can't bear the noise any longer. Have you seen the wood pile? We already have more firewood than we know what to do with. I suppose a certain amount of dead wood should be left in the forest to rot, don't you? I mean, for the balance of nature?"

"I suppose so," said Thomas. He disliked hearing Sarah babble like this. She had always tended to babble when she was nervous. At breakfast this morning she had been too bright, too full of chatter, too intent on drawing their attention to every bit of fur or feather that happened past the porch of the cottage— woodpeckers, hummingbirds, chipmunks, and on the lake off the end of the dock a pair of loons with two grayish, half-grown babies.

"Oh, aren't they dear!" Sarah had exclaimed, and she had insisted that each of them around the table take a turn with the binoculars. Thomas had had enormous trouble locating the birds on the swells of magnified water. One problem up here was the confusing light. Take now: the woods were broken up with too much dapple, the lake with too much motion and sparkle. And all those creatures Sarah was so fond of were forever darting and flitting and scurrying, next to impossible to catch with the eye when they were pointed out.

When he and Sarah reached the boathouse dock, Thomas was relieved to be able to breathe air that was coming to them from across the water. Another thing he disliked about the north woods was the closeness and moistness of them, so that it was impossible to take a breath without breathing in the decay of the woods. The trees looked like a fist around the lake, but at least over the water the air could pick up a little freshness and speed. He plumped down beside Sarah on the wooden bench, above the millions of tiny bright waves, wishing he had thought to bring his sunglasses in his shirt pocket. The setter had limped along the path after them and was now standing in the rocky shallows, slurping up some of the yellow-brown water.

"And so you did sleep well?" Sarah asked him for the second time.

"Yes, quite as well as can be expected in a strange bed." Actually he had been cold, but too drowsy to get up for another blanket, and the bed had been too soft, the pillow too hard and musty, and pressing in on him from outside had been a thicket of wild sounds, pierced through at unpredictable times by the wildest sound of all, the unrestrained laughing of the loon.

"I always have such deep sleeps when I come up here," said Sarah. "I leave everything behind, I forget city matters. I sleep like a baby."

Beside another man, Thomas refrained from saying. The loons were lucky, he thought, with that wild sound of theirs, which could cut right through everything.

He shielded his eyes with his hand, looked away from her, over the water, and said, "Well, you've brought some extra baggage along with you this time."

"And I'm delighted you came." She reached over and squeezed his knee quickly. "I knew you would, once Martha had worked on you."

"She did that, all right. She worked on me." He paused and squinted sideways at her. "And it sounds as if she has done a job on herself, too."

"So she told you then? I didn't know when she'd think the time was right."

"The time isn't right," said Thomas, "at least not in my opinion."

"I meant, the time to tell you. I think she was afraid you might bite her head off."

"Nonsense. I've always listened to her calmly. When have I ever stopped her from having her say?"

"What do you really think about the baby, Thomas?"

Thomas clamped his arms across his chest. "It's a fool notion."

"Is that what you said to her?"

"I don't remember exactly what I said to her. I asked her who was going to take care of it."

"And what did she say?" The red setter had now come clicking down the dock and was offering Sarah a paw, which she leaned forward to hold, muck and all.

"What did she say to *you*?" he demanded. "How long have you been in on this?"

"Not much longer than you, but she told me she has been thinking about it for a long time. She seems very determined to do this on her own. And she does seem to have some very good friends. Maybe she'll even marry the man one day."

"She is absurdly idealistic," said Thomas. "She's only imagining the good parts."

"And what are the good parts, Thomas?" Sarah's voice took on a sly note.

Thomas couldn't speak right away. He lowered his eyes against the terrible movement and brilliance of the water. "I'm no authority," he said finally.

"This will be our grandchild," said Sarah.

"We're not going to be around long enough to *be* grandparents, Sarah."

"Aren't we?"

Her glibness was like that shifty light on the water. "Speak for yourself," he said. "I do know enough to know my earthly limitations."

Sarah sighed and wiped her wet hand on the dog's back. "She's not going about this as I would have wished, either. But why shouldn't she have a chance? Why shouldn't she be able to try it her own way?"

"No one can stop her from trying whatever she wants. But

you asked me what I thought, and I'm telling you. The whole business is hard enough with two parents. That's what I told her, if you need to know the exact words. I said, It's hard enough with two."

"I asked her about a name," said Sarah. "A surname. I suppose it's silly, but that's the first thing I could think of to say. She says she's going to use my maiden name. I was very surprised. Somehow, that's the thing that is surprising me the most, Thomas. I don't see why she isn't considering her own name."

"She probably did," said Thomas, "and she probably decided that there was no meaning left in it."

"Well, of course there's meaning left in it! It's her own name, for heaven's sake. She's still Martha Burden."

"There's no meaning left in it," insisted Thomas, almost on top of her words. "You and I took the meaning out of that name, Sarah. I don't even like it much myself anymore. I might give it up for something else. Hardt. How does that sound? Thomas Hardt." He cocked a naughty eye on her—on her bright face, on her white hair held back today with a band of polka-dotted silk, tied into a ridiculous bow over one ear.

She was giving off a high, nervous laugh. "Thomas, you are letting yourself become a very strange man."

"I don't care anymore," he said. He stretched out his long legs and crossed one foot over the other.

"Of course you care, Thomas! You have just never let yourself admit how much you care."

"Is that so?" he said, with what he hoped was just the right amount of flatness.

Sarah took that moment to reach down again to the dog stretched out on the dock—a handsome dog, Thomas had to admit, with noble bone structure that even age couldn't ruin. "We should be talking about Martha, not ourselves," said Sarah.

"It's fate," said Thomas. "What could we say to change anything now? It's too late, Sarah."

Just at that moment the breakfast he had eaten lurched un-comfortably around a bend, and Thomas knew that he was in for some uneasy hours. The bacon had been a mistake. Maybe the orange juice, too. Acid was a mistake first thing in the morn-ing. Applesauce would have been better, but even applesauce wasn't always a certainty. But the bacon, that was the biggest mistake. Sarah never used to cook bacon in the morning. She must have started doing it for Otto, the protein lover.

"I don't know if it could be called fate, Thomas. Martha says she thought and thought about this, especially during all her travels last year. The idea was growing—maybe she didn't even know it herself for a long time."

"Fate—you see?" Thomas told her. "All you can do is watch it happen." He pressed a hand into his side. The day might come, he thought, when there would be nothing left on the face of the earth that he would be able to digest. Without food, you would die; with it, you could be so miserable you wanted to die. There ought to be a better way.

"Heads up," called out Martha's voice, and before Thomas could think, he had looked up and been photographed on a boat dock bench beside a former wife by a pregnant, unmarried daughter. She was leaning against a shoreline birch. "Beautiful light," she said to them across the water, "beautiful reflections."

"Then you surely don't need us to ruin the view," said Thomas. He heard the camera click several more times, and then Martha came the rest of the way along the path and onto the dock, where she stopped again and snapped the two of them, the grandparents, while Sarah's hands were still midair adjusting that silly bow in her hair.

"How now?" said Martha as she sauntered toward them. "I'd say you've found a pretty nice place to sit this morning. How's the water temperature?" She knelt near them and ran a hand through the water. "Not bad at all. Are we going to get you in the lake, Dad?"

"I don't have a bathing suit," he answered. "I'm not prepared for all this strenuous physical activity in the open air."

He almost liked the way Martha was laughing up at him from her crouched position. It reminded him how they had been conspirators, he and she, once upon a time—how they would sneak off to practice driving when Sarah was on the telephone, or slip away to movies at odd hours of day and night, or decide to eat nothing, say, but bananas and frozen custard when Sarah went to look after her ailing parents. *Do you remember the bananas and frozen custard?* he thought of saying to Martha now. *Do you remember the way we used to weave the car around under the bridge?* He wanted to say these things in front of Sarah. He wanted to say to Sarah herself, *You think the life all came from you, but it didn't, and you thought you were winning all the time, but you weren't, at least not always.*

And then to Martha he would say: *Where is he, this so-called father of your child, this alleged begetter?*

"Well, I intend to get you out in the boat, anyway," said Martha. "Why not now, right now?"

"It's awfully bright, isn't it?" said Thomas. "It's too dazzling."

Martha laughed again. To her mother she said, "Otto is making up the list for town and wants to confer with you. I'll take over here."

This is outrageous, thought Thomas, they have indeed made a case out of me. The two of them sounded like nurses changing shifts. He stood up. "Off I go for my morning nap," he said. "Good-bye, ladies, good night, ladies. It's that time."

And there was no time to lose, either, he realized, as he took a few steps and his innards contracted loathsomely.

"I won't take no for an answer," Martha called after him. "I'll get you out on the water sooner or later because it's just too beautiful to be missed."

Thomas heard them talking to each other as he walked up the path on heavy legs. He heard the car start and grind away down the gravel road as he sat suffering in the cramped guest bathroom at the back of the cottage. He watched a spider crawling near the drain of the metal shower stall. He heard a motor boat on the lake, somewhere out on the water dangerously far away from bathrooms. He thought it would be an appropriate moment for the world to end.

After lunch, during which he had refused everything but a cup of tea and a small bowl of Sarah's chicken soup, Thomas took up a book and settled himself in a rocking chair on the broad screened porch. Otto was in the adjacent main room, making a few telephone calls, something about an electrical system, something about an option to buy. It was impossible not to listen.

"See here, Norm," said Otto's forceful voice, "I have until Thursday to make up my mind. You tell him that. It's in writing. Tell him I can see right through what he's trying to do— no, don't tell him that."

Sarah had gone to take a nap. Thomas didn't know where Martha was. He tried to read a few pages of a fiction that, if someone were to ask him about it, he had just decided he would pronounce "specious." He came to the words *periodontal surgery* and stopped reading for a moment. He ran his tongue over his teeth, both natural and false, and over the sensitive areas where the gums were receding.

"What I was hoping you could do between now and then is find out if Mackey is really going in there with parking," said Otto. "As far as we're concerned, parking is the bottom line. If Mackey comes in, we'd be sitting pretty. Could you find out that much? All right. Okay, call me then."

Martha appeared outside on the porch steps. "Hey, there," she said softly to Thomas through the screen. "Now is a great time for the boat. What do you say?"

Otto had dialed another number. "Orville?" he said, as if to someone deaf. "Otto Hardt here. Do you think your son would like to come out here on Wednesday with his saw? I've still got some birches to clean up on the point."

Martha was scratching on the screen. "Let's make a get-away," she said.

Thomas snorted at her. "Aren't we a little old for shenanigans like that?"

"Never," whispered Martha. "Come on."

"You don't want me out there," said Thomas. "I might have to come home in a hurry."

"That's all right," said Martha. "Come *on*."

Otto gave off a short guffaw into the telephone. "You don't say!"

"All right," Thomas said to Martha, as if he had been spurred. "Wait a minute." He went to the bathroom and then got his hat and his dark glasses, walking twice past Otto, who lifted a friendly hand in greeting and went on talking, something about beaver on an island.

Thomas thought he could hear Sarah stirring behind her bedroom door at one end of the big room. Quickly he crossed the porch and let himself out.

Down in the boathouse, Martha was already lifting cushions and fishing gear into one of the smaller boats.

"I leave the luxury liner for Otto," she said. "This one is just my speed." It gratified Thomas how much she sounded like him at that moment, how unmistakably she was his daughter.

At the top of the vertical wooden ladder he hesitated. The boat bobbed below him. He didn't think he could do it. He stood looking down, remembering across seven decades to the twenty-foot vertical ladder that had plunged precipitously from the hay mow on his cousin's farm, remembering that each time he had had to swing his legs over for the first sheer steps, he had had a moment of death, and he had thought that death might be better than the ladder, better than his cousin's laughter below in the big central corridor of the barn, better than the dumb thudding of the beasts in their stalls.

"Take one step down and then go directly onto the seat of the boat," said Martha. She stood up from untying the boat and took his hand firmly, and suddenly he had done it.

"Three cheers," she said, and he couldn't tell if she was making fun of him or not. He composed himself on one of the middle plank seats while Martha made a few tries at starting the outboard motor. Not for the world would he have risked helping her. One old geezer in the lake—that's all they'd need—or with a wrenched back. He watched her breathe deeply and pull the starter rope again. She had definitely gained some weight. He studied her backside in the loose white shorts, the backs of her bare legs, the slight tracing of blue veins beneath the skin. The future child was mercifully still out of sight.

"I'm glad I'm not you," Thomas heard himself saying just as the motor caught and roared. Martha sat down facing him, raised her arm in a gesture of triumph, and began to back the boat out. He didn't know if she had heard him or not. Her mouth below the sunglasses had been painted with more lipstick than usual, and she was wearing harsh nail enamel, too. Female armor. He couldn't see why Martha of all people would think she needed it.

"Hold onto your hat," she told him loudly, and for a few minutes she drove full speed into the middle of the large lake, staying clear of the fishing boats stationed here and there. Now and then they pounded across the washboard waves of a speedboat, and Thomas gripped the edge of his seat with both hands, not enjoying himself. He was about to shout to her that he didn't think his spine could take any more jolting when she slowed, and the boat rocked in a slosh of sudden leisureliness.

"Do you see our boathouse?" Martha asked.

Thomas peered at the distant rim of trees. Even if Sarah were to search for him with her binoculars, it was doubtful that she would be able to make him out. And poor Miss Green could write a dozen notes, a hundred notes, and not one of them could reach him here. Thomas felt himself cradled for a moment in the pleasure of hiding out.

"It's there if you know how to look for it," said Martha, pointing. "There's a little bit of a dip in the trees just to the left of it."

Thomas shielded his eyes and looked again but could see no boathouse on the far shore. The door of it, he remembered, had been like a square black mouth as they had sped away. Sarah would have emerged from her nap by now and found them gone. She might even be waiting on the bench when they returned. Then he envisioned not Sarah on the bench in her cotton skirt with a scarf about her head and a dog at her feet, but an empty wooden bench, mute. He blinked. Sarah could die, before him, and he would return from his hiding place and find that he had been left behind.

"Never mind," said Martha. "Everything sort of blurs together when you're this far out. Shall we do any fishing?"

"Are there any fish to be caught?" he asked absently, still thinking of the empty bench. And what if he got back to town and found, as Martha had imagined, that poor Miss Green would have moved away? No more messages. He might, one day, find himself in opposition to no one at all.

Thomas leaned over the side of the boat, over the featureless shadow of a man in a hat, to see into the water if he could. "How deep is it?" he asked.

"Very," said Martha. "Otto could probably tell you exactly. I think he has the bottom of the lake memorized. He spent his summers on this lake, you know, when he was growing up."

"No, I didn't know that."

"His father built the cottage. Otto sort of idolized his father. I think it has been hard on Otto that he has never had any children of his own."

"Well, he has had some of you, hasn't he?"

"I was a little too old to start with," said Martha. She had taken up one of the fishing rods and was poking with a forefinger into a container of worms. "I was too old, and moreover I was the wrong sex." She said these words pointedly, and then she began to thread the worm onto the hook. "I was the wrong sex for him and I was the wrong sex for you."

"What are you talking about?" said Thomas as he accepted the handle of the baited line. "You sound as if you've been reading too many magazine articles. Having a daughter has been quite sufficient for me, thank you."

"Mother told me you didn't even want children."

"Sarah told you that? When did she tell you that?"

"Years ago, I don't remember exactly."

"Knowing you, I'd say you probably do remember exactly, time and place. Well, she shouldn't have told you. That was between the two of us, it had nothing to do with you."

Martha laughed outright and threw her own line into the water. After a minute or two of reeling it in, she said in a careful voice, "If you'd never had any children, do you think you two would still be married?"

Thomas just held his pole still, not casting. He was remembering that he had never particularly cared for fishing. The excitement that others seemed to anticipate he did not care about. The sun was very hot, too.

"I don't think this time of day is very good for fishing," he said. "The sun is too high."

"Other boats are out," said Martha. "Can you answer my question?"

"No," said Thomas, looking at her sidelong. "It's an unspeakable question. It's not good to press questions like that on a dying man."

"I'm sorry," said Martha, with no inflection of apology. "I didn't know you were dying."

Thomas found himself thinking about the bottom of the lake. What did she think it was like down there, he wanted to ask.

He brought up his line and looked at the logy worm. Then a dangling end of it moved, head or tail he could not tell. He sighed and let down the line again.

"Your mother had to have a child," he began to tell her before he realized that he was intending to speak. "Her desire seemed so much stronger, finally, than my own ideas that I acquiesced. I was up against something much larger than myself." He saw how Martha was sitting, one long bare leg curled on the seat against the gunwale, the other stretched out into the boat, side-saddle, more or less, with the fishing rod for reins, the white hat and sunglasses obscuring all of her face save the painted mouth. He said to her, "I believe you will understand what I mean when I say that a woman who wants to have a child is one of the strongest forces in the world. I may have been opinionative all my life, but at least I've known that everyone should be allowed to have his say."

"In this case, *her* say?"

"All right, have it your way, if you ladies want to go out and change the language along with everything else. I'm old enough that it's not going to affect me much, one way or another."

"Are you getting many bites on that line?" asked Martha abruptly.

"Nothing. I think the sun is too high."

"Pull in. I'm going to take you to one of my favorite places."

This time she started the motor right away. She shouted something at him with the red mouth and pointed to a place on the opposite shore. He had no idea what she had in mind. He gripped the seat again and prepared to go along with her. Luckily, his intestines were fairly quiet this afternoon, not many snarls on that dangerous highway below. He was having one of those rare moments, the closest he probably ever came to well-being these days, when he felt more or less empty of food.

There had been countless other times when he had wanted to pull his innards out entirely, just to get rid of the discomfort and foulness. Hadn't Martha been at all aware of what he was living through those years? He remembered taking Martha to a natural history museum one day when he had been particularly miserable with indigestion. Both of them had been held by the sight of a wizened mummy, its bandages partly pulled back from the black, grimacing face, the tight body perfectly still, emptied of its pulp—though filled with sawdust probably—waiting for a better life. For Martha the fascination had most likely been with gruesomeness itself, but for him at the moment the idea had come that a better life might indeed emerge out of stillness and emptiness, that the Egyptians might have been going in the right direction, even if they had interpreted it too literally. He wondered if that day Martha had had any glimmering that the father beside her wanted only to be reamed out and left alone to recover from the shock of having been born.

Thomas reached out a hand to touch the hard leaping spray beside the boat. It was difficult not to think literally if you had to live in a body. Yeats was right: didn't all dreams of the soul always return to the body? What sort of emptiness could ever be possible? And look at Martha, deliberately filling herself up with a child. What would it be like, to have the inside of you taken over, incredibly distorted by a baby? It was unthinkable.

Martha had just cut the motor and was guiding the boat alongside a small, listing dock, on top of a submerged metal track that was slanting up out of the water toward a crude winch. Ahead of them, channeling straight into the forest, was a long, dark avenue of water, at the other end of it an entrance to more sunlight.

"Where are we?" he asked.

"I'm taking you over to Diamond Lake. Home of the local leviathan."

"Is this the only way to get there?"

"Only way. Diamond is tiny, in the middle of nowhere. But you'll have to get out of the boat, Dad, so we can pull it up to the channel."

"You're asking a great deal."

Martha was already on the dock, reaching a hand toward him. "You'll do it," she said, and he did. He even obeyed her instructions and turned the crank on the winch a few times so that Martha could steady the boat in the cradle frame as it rose out of the water and creaked up the track to the cement dam. "Hold it there," she said, "you're doing fine," and she hurried around him to the dock on the canal side and pulled the boat into the quiet darker water. Thomas took off his hat and wiped his head and neck with his folded handkerchief.

"If you'll excuse me, I think I should take a little walk," he said.

"I will, too," said Martha as she knotted the boat around a post.

Separately they stepped into the pine-scented woods. Thomas chose a large tree not far from the top edge of the sandy bank. Urination was easy enough. He felt grateful that for now no more was necessary. Somewhere behind him, off to his right where he had heard sticks breaking beneath her steps, Martha would be turning herself into a humble squatting female for her own performance. Thomas waited for a few moments, upright, looking out over the lake. A small wind blew against him.

He looked at the line after line of motion in the waves below. Before long he would have to face dinner, and digestion would begin all over again. Before he could sleep, he would have to talk with the others in little waves of sound, wave after wave of thoughts and words building up, leaving traces. Then he would have to brush his teeth, the same old teeth, and wash himself.

"What do you see?" asked Martha, coming up from behind.

"Waves," he answered. "And dinner."

"Dinner? Are you wishing we'd really catch some fish?"

"Not that, exactly," he said, "but I suppose it wouldn't be such a bad thing to come home with something to show."

"Then let's go have a try at Diamond Lake. Otto really does

believe that an enormous fish is down there somewhere. Once when he was a boy he caught a small fish on this lake and carried it in a bucket through the woods to Diamond—the canal wasn't built then—and dumped it in and told it to grow."

"Otto's quite the one for long-range planning, isn't he?"

"There are things that have happened around him that I'm sure he would have planned against if he could have."

"Like the death of his first wife, you mean?" asked Thomas.

"That, of course, but then there was his sister Ginnie—did you know about her? The one who killed herself?"

"You must remember," said Thomas with a gathering of his dignity, "that your mother and I have not had all that much commerce these past years—certainly not enough for me to know or care about the various members of Otto's family."

Martha took his arm. "I'm sorry," she said. "Let's go catch our fish."

This time Thomas sat himself on the edge of the dock, swung his legs into the boat, and managed in that way to embark without assistance. They slid off into the shaded canal. Thomas could see to the bottom of the water, down to the weeds and sunken leaves and crisscrossed branches, fuzzy with disintegration. He watched himself gliding backwards over those accumulated layers of matter and over this year's new weeds that next winter would be bent and then flattened by the descending ice.

Martha had set the motor on the lowest speed. Leaning over the edge of the boat, Thomas began to feel almost dreamy with watching all they were passing over. He hoped Martha would not start talking right away.

"How's your neck today?" she asked.

"I haven't been thinking much about it."

"That's a good sign," said Martha. "I should be giving you some of my famous neck rubs. I'm getting very good at them."

"Is that so?" He tried to make his voice pleasant and neutral, but now he had been set to wondering about those necks she must have been rubbing in that life of hers he knew so little about. He sat upright, no longer soothed by the passing underwater life of the canal. The necks of which men? What sort of man would agree to such a thing, fathering a child without being in a position to father it? In spite of all his own faults, Thomas thought, at least he had known that a child deserved an available father and a father's name. He frowned sternly into the forest that grew down to the edge of the canal. Now, absurdly, without his having anything to say about it, with no regard to his own principles, he was being asked to be an available grandfather.

He was just about to open his mouth and force her to admit what an absurdity it was, this child—*apropos the subject of long-range planning,* he would begin—when she said to him, "Dad, do you think you've always had a delicate constitution?"

"Why do you ask that?"

"I've never heard you say what your health was like when you were a child."

"It's hard to compare those days with these," he told her. "And our town was so pitifully small. We went through periods of not even having a doctor."

"Really?" He saw her adjust her weight on the plank seat; he saw how the hand that was not steering the boat she now placed on her abdomen. He saw this, and he saw that there was nothing he could do to stop what had been begun.

"Yes, really," he said. "A lot of people doctored themselves. My mother was always anxious about my health, especially after I had rheumatic fever. I suppose I had more than my share of upsets. My digestion has always been very unstable. It has been an annoyance to me for as long as I can remember. I get worn out living with it." He eyed her askance—he didn't want her to laugh at him. "I really think I'd like to find a way not to have to eat."

Martha laughed. "I love to eat. I'm a pig. Right now I'm thinking about that rye bread we didn't finish at lunch and how I'm going to spread some with cream cheese as soon as we get back."

"Was it good?" asked Thomas. "I didn't feel up to it."

"Excellent. Very solid and healthy-tasting."

"Hmm," said Thomas. "I haven't had good rye bread in quite a while."

"You can join me," said Martha. "We can sit down on the porch swing and eat up all the rye bread together."

"I guess we had a few crazy meals together in the old days, didn't we?"

"Great meals, just great," said Martha. "Do you remember the bananas and frozen custard? You were a child after my own heart, Dad."

Thomas clapped his hat on his head because just then the boat slipped out upon the sun-shot, round pool of Diamond Lake. Having gone backwards down the canal, he was almost astonished by the moment. It was amazing that such a self-contained, almost perfectly round little lake should be hidden in the forest. When they had reached the center, Martha shut down the motor and they began to drift slowly. Thomas turned on his seat to take in the whole circle. There was not much to notice except trees, upright and fallen at odd angles along the shore and into the water. As Martha fitted the oars into the locks, the sound of metal on metal reverberated in the clearing.

She handed Thomas his fishing pole. "Otto recommends fly fishing in here, but I guess I didn't bring along the right gear. I really don't know how to do it anyway, do you?"

"No," said Thomas. "I've never really cared that much for fishing."

"I know you haven't! Do you remember that summer we rented a cottage, and Mother and I ended up going out in the boat together every day while you read on the dock?"

"I always had too much to read," said Thomas. "There was no end to it."

"But you must have liked it," pressed Martha.

"Oh, there are moments. One of the best for me was when I discovered Traynor—I know I've told you this. It happened that same summer I proposed to Sarah, almost at the same time. Funny, isn't it? I picked up this book by a guy named William Traynor just for something to read while Sarah was on a little trip—she was making up her mind, you see, whether she'd have me or not. I started reading about eleven in the morning—I'll never forget that day—and it was all I could do to make myself get up and find something to eat at six o'clock. Cold chicken. I've never had another meal that tasted like that—sublime. I knew I was onto something big. No one was talking about William Traynor. I knew he was buried treasure, and I was going to be one of the first voices coming out for him. I read almost until midnight before the book was done, but I couldn't sleep for the rest of the night. By noon the next day your mother had called, and I knew I had not just Traynor, but your mother, too."

Thomas looked away from his daughter and frowned. "Well, there are always moments," he said. "But most of the time you have to wait so long for them. And the problem with my work was that I had to be vigilant all the time. It wears you out, all that discrimination."

It annoyed him that Martha said nothing now, but just cast her line out and slowly began to reel it in. His own he had simply plopped into the water, with the same old worm, and he sat above it now under a sun that felt like a spotlight.

"A critic has to have a vision," he began to say, and then paused. "And he has to extend that vision. He has a responsibility to stamp out what is irresponsible, what is really bad."

White hat, sunglasses, red mouth: Martha was turning to him, and finally she said, "I'm afraid that if I had a job like that I'd always try to find something good to say. I'd be afraid of being haunted by my remarks. I've always wondered how you could do it."

"Look here," said Thomas, "there's too much that's shoddy everywhere. We're surrounded by what's inferior. Hunting too hard for something good to say is wrongheadedness, I think. There's no way that overwhelming badness can be redeemed by small felicities. Certainly I've always tried to be fair, but I've had high standards when it comes to books. Someone has to. It's a shoddy marketplace, let's face it."

"Sometimes I buy a paperback at the grocery store and read it late at night," said Martha. "It's like taking the wrapper off a candy bar. The gooier the better, once you've made the decision to indulge."

Thomas sighed. The top of his pole was nearly touching the water now, but he didn't feel he had the will to hold it properly. Martha's words had given him an image of her car, strewn with the detritus of her haphazard habits, and then of her bedroom, though he had not actually seen her present apartment. He imagined books and candy wrappers in the bed covers, photographic prints everywhere, dusty, with curling edges, coffee cups, soft drink cans. And now there would be boxes of crackers, too, and half-drunk glasses of milk. And soon little heaps of diapers . . .

"Next time you're buying paperback books," he said to her, "you'd better pick up a few on how to be a parent alone. Don't they have a catchy way to say it these days?"

"Single Parenting," said Martha.

"That's it," said Thomas. "I think you'd better do some homework, my girl. I think you're going to need it. I'm glad I'm not the one having this baby." He thought of the work that was ahead of her, the years and years of woman's work, coming out of woman's body.

"Say there!" he cried, for there had been some sharp tugs on his line, sending a sort of electricity all the way up the pole and into him. "I think I've got a fish interested. I'm feeling something. Wouldn't that be funny, after the desultory way I've been fishing?" He held the pole carefully now, waiting.

"It would be a scream," said Martha.

"What shall I do now," he asked. "Just hold still?"

Martha said nothing.

"Do you think he got my worm?" asked Thomas. "I wouldn't have wanted that worm if I were a fish." He waited a minute more and then reeled up the line. The hook was empty. "The little devil," he said. He was warming up to the idea of catching that particular fish. "Hand me the container of worms, will you, Martha? He's probably right down there under the boat. I'll show him."

Martha did not hand him the container of worms. Her dark glasses were turned on him again. "Dad, why did you do it to her?" she said to him in a voice so low it seemed to cancel out everything else.

He had been struck. The little excitement over the fish instantly drained away, and he felt very old as he sat there balancing the pole against his leg and awkwardly holding the wet, empty line. "Why did I do what?" he asked her. "What are we talking about?"

He could barely see her. His eyes must not be working properly. He wanted to beg her to stop making him say all these words.

"We're talking about Mother," said Martha, but this time her voice broke. "We're always talking about Mother, no matter what else we're talking about, don't you know that? You left her—"

"I did not! She left *me*. Please think, Martha!"

"—you left her alone, you left her so much that when she finally left you there was nothing to leave. I know! I have been *thinking*. What do you think I've been doing all these years? I know, I know."

He was mortified for her. He had not seen her cry like this since she was a child. He was mortified for himself. "Martha, this much sun is not good for either of us. I'm not feeling at all well, and you certainly don't sound like yourself."

"Would you like to tell me to go to my room and get control of myself? Is that what you're trying to say?"

"Yes, I would," he said. "At least row us over to the canal where we can get some shade. I think we're both sunstruck."

"Don't you want to catch your fish," she said unpleasantly, her voice still catching.

"I don't care a damn about fishing, you know that. Please get us out of here." He set down his pole and waited. He was reminded of her stubbornness as a child, how the only way through it sometimes was to wait her out. Once, when her breathing had stopped during a tantrum, her big toes had curled rigidly upward and become locked in that position, and when she had noticed this and pointed down in horror, still speechless, he had said, See? See what happens to little girls who make such a fuss? or something like that, and most likely he would have walked from the room. I don't have to listen to any more of this, he would sometimes say to her. Or to Sarah: I am not required to listen to this. They had no idea how ridiculous they could sound.

Martha blew her nose savagely and then lifted the oars out over the water, but she did not begin to row. She leaned forward, no longer crying. "You left her alone. What I'm asking you is if you had any idea what you were doing when you left her alone."

"You're talking nonsense. I gave her what she wanted. She wanted a child: I gave her a child. You! She wanted to build a new house: I built a new house. Two houses, damn it! I worked myself silly for those houses, and who's living in them now? Strangers. All that work. And where is Sarah living? She's living in a house she got another man to build. Do *you* have any idea what I'm saying to *you?*"

"Of course I do—who do you think I am? But what I think is that maybe almost from the very beginning you somehow left her alone, you put her off to one side of your mind. You said that she wasn't worth thinking about."

"I don't know where you get these ideas of yours," he said. "A man doesn't do that to a woman—a woman's at the center. But a man has to be on the move, he has to go places. He can't think about a woman all the time. Everything would fall to pieces, nothing would get done."

"That's not what I mean."

"I don't understand you," said Thomas. "I think I started out adoring your mother. I took her under my arm, I couldn't believe my good fortune. But I had to look out for provisions. I had to find out enough about myself to face what had to be done. A man can't look to a woman for that, he's got to look to himself. And those were the old days, Martha. Remember that."

Thomas heard that his voice had begun to plead, but he couldn't stop himself. "Picture it. There was Sarah. She wanted a child, she wanted a house. You don't know what you're talking about. In order to get her the things she wanted, I had to put my mind to the task."

Martha had slowly begun rowing back toward the canal. Thomas felt terribly agitated. He didn't like what was happening. "All right," he said. "Maybe I was frightened of some things, maybe I wasn't wholehearted enough, but who is? Who knows what is really important and goes straight for it? I was experimenting. You say I didn't want a child. All right, maybe at first I didn't. Maybe I was trying to save my child from being born. Maybe I was trying to save my child from *this*." He found himself stabbing in the troubled air between them. He didn't like the set of her mouth and the way she kept on silently rowing. "You're not the one to talk anyway," he said. "Look at you: look at who's frightened. I don't see you getting married. Oh no, you've got some better way—is that it?"

"I'm experimenting," said Martha. She was regaining her composure, but Thomas didn't know if he wanted her to or not, with him being still so rattled. He tipped his hat brim even lower. When they had once more reached the shade of the canal, she reached under her seat and from a heap of life jackets brought out a canteen and a box of crackers. She passed him the canteen.

"Thank you," said Thomas. His hand was shaking as he struggled with the cap. He was appalled at how upset he had let himself become. For weeks there had been nothing but upset after damnable upset, either from his unreliable body, or from that untrustworthy Miss Green, or sometimes just from his own galling thoughts about what a fool he had been to believe even for a moment that there was still some sweetness in Sarah intended for him. All this was a crazy business. He was losing his judgment, his reserve. Anything could get to him now. He had even forgotten how to speak in a civilized way—and how often had he himself held forth on the importance of relations between people being clothed in decent words. He was appalled at the baldness of how he and Martha had been speaking.

Finally he managed to get the canteen open, and as he tipped back his head to drink, some of the water spilled down his chin and the front of his shirt. He hadn't realized how thirsty he was.

"I'll tell you what I think," said Martha around a mouthful of cracker. "I think that you're just not all that interested in the subtleties of female experience."

He stopped drinking and looked at her in horror. She was speaking an unconscionable gobbledy gook. He poured a little water in his hand and wiped it over his hot face and the back of his neck. He wasn't even intending to answer her, but then he said, "For a smart girl, you're using a great deal of jargon. I don't think I raised you to talk like that."

"Oh?" said Martha. "How did you raise me?"

He passed the canteen back to her. "On second thought, maybe I should leave the credit to your mother."

"Maybe you should," said Martha. He didn't like her smoothness. He felt dismissed.

"I'd like to know who's going to take care of that baby of yours when you're off taking pictures of everyone else. You're not going to be the kind of mother your mother was, that's obvious."

"I've been thinking about that," said Martha.

He shook his head. "You don't know what's ahead. For example, do you know what pride your mother took in being there when you got home from school? I don't believe she missed a single day until you were in high school and her own parents began to fail and needed her. It was very nearly a perfect record, Martha. Think about what that means."

"I have been," she said. "For a long time."

Shadows were slipping over her as she rowed down the canal. In the midst of the forest their words had begun to sound softened. For a few minutes they were silent, and Thomas felt some of the agitation pass out of him. With tired eyes he watched Martha slowly bend and pull, bend and pull on the oars. He thought the silence was probably a good thing. Could it be just words that were the cause of all this distress between people? He pressed a hand on his chest and drowsily watching his daughter rowing him back the way they had come. Then he said to her, "I suppose you're going to turn up now and then and expect me to act like a grandfather?"

"Yes, I'd like that," said Martha.

"I should have been consulted," he said.

He thought he saw her smile before he closed his eyes and let his head drop to his chest. Then she began speaking again, a whole paragraph having something to do with a house and a garden. Her words fell into his mind like bits of type in the composing room, sounds becoming black marks marking the familiar vertical rectangle of a paragraph. Then he was walking into a narrow green room that he had expected to be full, but only three people were in the very last chairs, waiting to take notes on what he would say. Was this all the attention he deserved? Suddenly he realized that he had no notes for a speech. He was not prepared to say anything at all.

The boat bumped hard against the dock. "Here we go again, Dad." Martha sounded tired, too. In a daze of fatigue he clambered out and helped her ease the boat down into the big lake. The wind had picked up. The boat knocked against the dock until Martha finally got the motor started. As they pounded across the choppy water, all the abrading words they had been speaking to each other shook together in his mind; he wished he could open his mouth and get rid of all of them over the side of the boat, let them fall to the bottom of the lake. Nothing meant enough. He endured the ride home with his eyes closed, his chin bumping against his chest.

The four of them were beginning to fall into small routines. Before dinner Thomas went to his room for a rest, as he had the evening before. He lay down on top of the bedspread and covered himself with the same green wool blanket. Beside him the window was open, and just beyond the mesh of rusted screen were the branches of a pine tree. Creatures of some sort, chipmunks probably, were rustling at its base. He didn't lift his head to look down on them. From high a bird now and then gave out a silvery whistle, which he remembered hearing the day before at this time. The clear sound fell freely from the sky, as if it had been shaken out over the cabin. Thomas did not sleep, but as he listened for repetitions of the bird call, he began to be relieved of the weight of his body. He began to be relieved of the jumbled echoes of all he and Martha had been saying that afternoon.

As they had been coming up the path from the boathouse, Martha had said to him, "Thank you for talking," and she had

kissed him on the cheek. He didn't think he deserved that, but
nevertheless there it was, a kiss. Thomas thought he could still
feel the place where her lips had touched. His feet and legs on
the bed were weightless, his hands were like huge balloons, his
breath was sieving finely in and out, but the place on his right
cheek was warm with the recalled light pressure of her lips. For
this moment he allowed himself to think that he was just an
ordinary man, with no more faults than anyone else, taking an
afternoon rest in the bosom of his family.

He rested until he heard a gathering of voices somewhere in
the common rooms. He found the three of them in the kitchen,
fixing themselves drinks.

Otto raised an empty glass toward Thomas. "Sparkling water
again, Thomas, or would you like something stronger?"

"Just the water, thank you," said Thomas. "I won't court
trouble."

"Rye bread, Dad?" asked Martha. She held out a segment,
already spread with cream cheese. Thomas eyed it carefully.

"All right," he said.

Something cooking on the top of the stove smelled delicious.
Sarah was lifting a lid and stirring. Thomas ventured to take a
look with her inside the pot.

"Lamb stew, Thomas," she said.

"It smells very good," said Thomas. He took a small bite of
the bread and began to chew. Sarah had changed her clothes,
he noticed. She had taken off the polka-dotted scarf and brushed
the waves of white hair high on her forehead. Now she wore a
pair of tan slacks and a white blouse and a navy blue cardigan.
Around her was a pool of rich scents, stew and perfume and
bourbon.

"I think we can sit on the porch now," said Sarah. "Everything is under control." Her nervousness of the morning had
passed into what appeared to be contentment. She was finally
getting what she wanted, he thought, this chance to fuss a little

over all of them together. If she had her way, she'd probably gather in everyone she cared about, just to see if something magical would happen between them. Thomas's body gave a shudder of sorts, he didn't know what it was.

"Thomas, would you like a jacket over your sweater?" asked Sarah. "There are plenty of old jackets in that big closet."

"No, no," he said. "I'm quite all right."

Martha's legs were still bare, but she had put on a large tan sweater that looked as if it had belonged to a man. He wanted to ask her about it, but didn't know how. He wanted to find this man and say to him, *Wait a minute, where do you think you're going?* Martha lay full length on the padded porch swing, her head propped up just enough so that she could take sips from her glass.

Thomas sat in one of the rocking chairs. "What's that you're drinking?" he asked. "I hope you don't have bourbon in that glass."

"It's ginger ale, Dad. See?" She held up the glass so that he could see the bubbles. Then she reached out with a bare foot and playfully set his chair in motion.

"That's wise of you," said Thomas. He cleared his throat. "From what I've read, babies and alcohol don't mix."

There was a small moment in which Thomas realized this was the first time the baby had been placed in the middle of the four of them. He was surprised at himself.

"Why, Thomas, what have you been reading?" asked Sarah in a pleased voice.

"I don't recall," he said. "The newspaper, most likely. I read in such an unsystematic way these days that I couldn't tell you where I've picked up one thing or another. I'm no longer being held accountable for anything, thank heaven."

"A lot different from the old days, no doubt," said Otto.

"Yes, quite different." A year ago Thomas had scarcely spoken a hundred words with Otto. Now, this was happening.

"Myself, I read for the gist," said Otto. "I don't have time for every word, never have. You fellows who give a good review save us a lot of trouble, do you know that? Many is the time I've finished with the newspaper and thought, Well, that's all I need to know about that." He sat with his stocky legs broadly planted. One large freckled hand was gripped around his bourbon, the other rested in a fist on his knee.

Otto's comment was what Thomas might have expected, but instead of countering it, he took a drink of his water and let his gaze stretch past Otto, through the birch and pine trees, far out over the lake. A thousand books more or less: what did it matter? What did he himself have, after all those years and all those books? The corners of his mouth turned down, and he saw the lake through watery eyes.

When they stood for dinner, Thomas was surprised how tall he was. He rose above Otto and Sarah, even above Martha. The bourbon drinkers had become a trifle ebullient. Beside them, Thomas felt sober and almost fatherly. He looked over worriedly at how Sarah had to steady herself beside her chair before she limped toward the table. She and Martha were laughing about what could be expected from the next day's Fourth of July parade. Thomas simply had to make the effort to come into town with them, they said.

Sarah set her unfinished bourbon beside her plate. "You must at least take a look, Thomas," she said. "You wouldn't want to miss the Muskie Queen."

"Or the John Birch Society," urged Martha. "Indians in war bonnets, drum and bugle corps, the Aqualand Princesses—think of it, Dad."

"I'm thinking, I'm thinking," said Thomas. "I'll wait until tomorrow to see how much static I'm feeling." He lowered the length of himself into one of the wicker chairs at the porch table and eyed Sarah's glass of liquor beside him. She never used to drink bourbon. In the old days she would sometimes have a sherry or a glass of wine while he had his nightly Scotch—that is, before the doctor took away his favorite palliatives—but now, she was drinking bourbon each night, with Otto. Thomas wondered if the alcohol could be doing her harm, so soon after her accident. It must take the body a long time to heal after a blow like that. She still complained of pain; maybe she always would have some. At their stage in life—his and Sarah's and Otto's—it was probably ridiculous to think about complete recovery, about any kind of perfection. It was probably ridiculous at any stage in life.

He frowned down at his plate, on which a painted pheasant flew upward in alarm. Years ago, he had really thought Sarah would become a different sort of person. And how to account for himself? His own path: was that what he had said he was looking for all those years? He almost snorted. What words people used with themselves! No one knew anything. Let her have her bourbon, and let her be married to Otto and have her pretty life, if that was what she wanted. She was probably better off this way.

Sarah was covering his painted pheasant with some of the stew. Then she dipped into the pot again and appeared to be careful in selecting the next spoonful. More vegetables were lowered onto his plate. "I guarantee that you'll get no static from *this* stew," she said. "I've put a good spell on it."

"I don't doubt that you could do it, my dear. I don't doubt it at all."

Thomas began to eat. Why shouldn't he call her *dear?* Hadn't he known her longer than either of the others? He had discovered her, for heaven's sake. He took another bite and another, and then he found the stew so delicious that he gave himself over to eating.

In the middle of the night Thomas woke abruptly, not with digestive trouble, but with a nameless alarm. His heart was beating too rapidly. He could not remember what he had been dreaming. The weather sounded as if it had changed. He let up the window shade and looked out into the swaying feathered blackness that was the pine tree. The wind had picked up. Just as he pulled the shade back down, the loons began to call and laugh wildly to each other. Thomas slid under the covers, as if he himself had caused the birds to cry out. One of the loons gave out another piercing laugh.

After a time, when he had not fallen asleep again, he sat up and turned on the bedside light. Two o'clock. His heart was still beating too rapidly. One by one he looked at the pictures on the wall of his room—more birds, an embroidered toad crouched beneath an embroidered mushroom, several framed cartoons about fishing: an ordinary cottage room where several generations of Otto's family had slept away summer nights. Maybe Otto had had a nicer family than most; maybe that was why it seemed easier for him to be kind.

Thomas lay down again on the lamp-lit pillow and tried to think only about quieting his heart and his breathing. Otto appeared to be healthier than most people, too. Every day he got up and went about his business—real business, with schemes and waiting periods and papers to sign and money coming in. Otto could get away with talking about the "bottom line" and the "gist" because he came through with the projects and the money—and the delivery of food baskets. He went along with life; he paid enough attention to please the people around him, apparently. Thomas frowned. By Otto's own admission he slept "like a top" every night. How was that possible? How about when his first wife was so sick: had he slept like a top while she was dying? And what about after Sarah's accident, when she lay with broken ribs and crushed leg and those frightening bruises under her eyes?

Sarah had lain like that for a week before Thomas even knew about the accident, before she sent for him and said, "Thomas, I have been thinking, it is time now, high time."

Thomas lifted an arm to shield his eyes from the lamp light, hearing her voice repeating those words, and then he felt a tightness in his chest, an ache in his throat and chest. He ached all over. He turned on his side and drew up his knees. He bit down on a wadding of sheet. And then he began to cry in convulsive gulps. He was devouring air and heaving it back out in gasps of hurt. Was it true what Martha had accused him of, that he had left Sarah alone, had in some essential way withheld himself? She had been right there, all those years right within touching. How had it happened that he had thought he had to set himself against her? Why had they been in such a jealous contest? He had adored her. How could he have denied her? He had just been doing what he thought he had to do. Oh, oh, what had both of them done!

In the morning light Thomas was surprised to be waking from a deep sleep. He still tasted the fullness of his sleep; his whole body felt swollen with it. He opened the window shade and saw that now the pine tree dripped with rain. The wind had died down, but inside the room a damp chill had settled. Thomas wished Sarah would take it into her head to come into his room and sit on the edge of the bed and tell him something, he didn't care what, just something to help him cross over into day. She would be wearing her navy blue sweater. She would take his hand and rub his knuckles between her fingers, and she would say some small things: it was just the sound of her voice he wanted.

And what he wanted now was to grasp her hand in return and say the one thing he had been storing up for her, the only wealth he had known how to amass, absurd and invisible as it was, and she could have it now, even through words she could take it from him now: he had been faithful to her, he needed to say; he had taken no women to his rooms, no men, had gone

to no other rooms. Only, alone in his own simple room, re-
signed; he had from time to time taken on the rueful celebration
of his own sex.

He wanted to hold tight to her hand and confess to her that
he had not started out intending this sort of chastity, but then
when he had realized that it was happening anyway, he had
begun to hold to it as an ideal, one small possible honor left,
one small opening through which he could pass and perhaps
emerge transformed. And then he would smile at her, shrug,
and say that of course it hadn't worked, it had been as absurd
as all his other ideas, but he wanted her to have it nevertheless:
he wished she would take it from him now.

Voices had begun coming to him from the big room and a
thudding that sounded like a fire being laid. Now there was the
clink of dishes. Thomas could wait no longer for someone who
was not coming. He got up and washed and shaved. He put on
a clean shirt and the same trousers and sweater. He made the
bed, not very neatly, and folded the extra green blanket. Then
he sat down to put on his socks and shoes. His toes looked
almost purple—not pretty feet, but his own. He leaned over to
clothe them, and in that instant the tears of the night before
returned. He crossed his arms over his middle and rocked for-
wards and backwards, trying to make as little sound as possible.
In a minute or two it was over. He shook his head and blew his
nose. He had had decades of solitary confinement for these
tears, why should they be coming now? Thomas, Thomas,
Sarah would say, it is time, high time.

When he was finally ready to face the rest of them, the first
of the logs in the fireplace had already collapsed, and Otto was
bending over adding new ones. Martha stood looking on—staring, really—and chewing on a piece of toast. Against the fire-
light Thomas saw her profile—like his and then not at all like
his. She was Martha.

She turned. "Hello, Dad. How are you?"

"As well as can be expected," he said and then wished he could have thought of words more original to this particular morning and to the picture he had had just now of her, Martha herself.

"Good morning, Thomas!" Otto was brushing off his hands, and Thomas thought for a moment that one of them might actually be extended toward him for a hearty shake, but Otto just said, "How do you like this Fourth of July weather? It's not what I ordered, let me tell you."

"I heard the wind change in the night," said Thomas, and he wished he would say more about the night, but he did not know how.

"Is that Thomas?" Sarah was looking around the corner of the kitchen door. The setter lay across the opening at her feet. "Good morning, Thomas. I've made some lovely oatmeal here —does that sound good to you?"

"Yes," he said. "Very good. It will be a change from my usual Cream of Wheat." The absurdity of who he was in this context caught in his voice.

Sarah must have heard it, for she said to him, "Please come help me carry these trays, Thomas. I think we're all ready."

He helped her carry the bowls of oatmeal, a basket of toast, bananas, jam, honey, tea, coffee for Otto. The table by the fire looked almost too nice. Thomas felt he deserved none of it; in a moment the rest of them would see how he did not belong, how unsuited he was to a pretty breakfast in front of a fire. If he could find a way—the bus, maybe—he would leave today, before they could start wishing in earnest that he had never come.

"Bless you," said Otto to Sarah. "This is just the breakfast we need on a morning like this."

Bless you? Thomas wondered if he had ever said words like that to Sarah. Was that how Otto managed her, got her to do what he wanted? Or was she the one directing him? It was difficult to tell. "Where do you want to sit, Thomas?" she was asking him. "Do you want your back to the fire?"

Martha had already taken a chair and was helping herself to more toast. "Something about this weather is making me awfully hungry," she said. "What will we do today? Does anyone want to brave the parade?"

"Oh, the parade!" exclaimed Sarah. "What will our poor Muskie Queen do today?"

"I should think she'd be right in her element," said Thomas suddenly.

Everyone laughed—a curious sound, that laughter, in such a small wooden space, with all the doors and windows closed against the rain.

"Bravo!" said Martha. "What do we need a parade for, with a group like this? We could play games. I haven't played cards in ages. Do you remember our rummy matches, Dad? You'd hold everything in your hand until the end, do you remember? You always wanted to surprise me with what you had been saving up."

"But then you'd go out on me," said Thomas. "She'd go out, you see," he explained to Otto, "and leave me with all these points against me. She had a way of knowing just how to catch me."

"Cards it will be, then!" said Otto. "I'm always game for cards. Sarah can get me to muddle through a few hands of bridge, but rummy and poker are still my favorites, sometimes hearts. Now there's a pretty good game. Let's see, do you pass the ones you don't want to the person on the right or the person on the left?" He gestured to Thomas and then to Sarah.

The telephone rang. "I'll get it," said Otto. "That will most likely be Orville about the chainsawing tomorrow."

The rest of them kept on eating. Sarah stirred and stirred a spoonful of sugar into her tea. "I had forgotten how you two would go after those cards," she said beneath the boom of Otto's voice. "Especially when one of you was sick. You had games that ran for days, didn't you?"

"Yes, forever," said Martha. "I could never get him to admit when he had lost."

"Not true!" said Thomas. "You were the one who kept raising the limit. You never wanted the game to end. Go to five hundred, you'd beg, go to seven-fifty."

"Well," said Sarah. "And what was I doing do you think when all these games were going on?"

"Talking on the telephone!" Thomas and Martha said nearly together.

"Was I? That much?"

"Yes, that much," said Martha. "I used to tell my friends that my mother had much better connections than I did." Thomas laughed at her, his girl.

Otto's telephone voice had lost its joviality. "Are you sure, Norm? Do you have the right building?"

Sarah held her cup of tea with both hands. "The things you find out about yourself," she said. "I don't know how I could have thought I had enough to say for all those conversations."

"The telephone was your umbilical cord," said Thomas suddenly. "It was your lifeline."

Sarah raised an eyebrow and looked at him over her cup. He looked back right into her eyes, through the curl of tea steam, his Sarah—as much his as anyone's.

They were all becoming aware now that Otto was upset and was trying to get something straight. "You've seen it for yourself, then?" he said. "Was anyone hurt? Can you get a handle on the damages somehow? It will make a difference to us here, what step we take next. All right. Yes, we'll be here all day." He hung up. He came back and stood by the fire. "Damnedest thing. There's been a fire, Thomas, in your building. Serious. That was my partner Norman. He saw it on the morning news and went over to have a look. We've got property on that block,

you know. He says it looks bad, the top floors at least. That's
your apartment and a few others. He heard rumors, but doesn't
really know how bad it is. Damnedest thing."

Thomas had pushed back his chair. "Last night?" he asked
Otto.

"Sometime in the early morning," said Otto. "Norm couldn't
find anyone who really knew the details, but he knows you're
with us, and I've pointed out your building to him. To tell the
truth, we've sort of had our eyes on it ourselves."

"Not that building!" said Thomas.

"Damnedest thing," said Otto. He sat down again and
reached for the jam. "Well, that's one way to get some major
repairs done. I'm very sorry for you, though, Thomas."

"But your things," said Sarah, "all your books and that beautiful library table of your father's. Is there someone you can call
to find out about your things?"

Martha put her hand on his arm. "Dad, maybe it was that
girl."

"What girl?" asked Sarah.

Thomas stared at Martha. "How do you think it could be that
poor girl?"

"I just do."

"What girl are you talking about?" demanded Sarah.
"Thomas? Martha?"

Martha turned to her mother. "She's an unhappy woman who
lives across the hall from Dad. We'll tell you . . . Dad, you could
call someone, couldn't you? The superintendent?"

"Billy," he said. "Billy Rea."

"Could you call him?" asked Martha. "Do you want me to
call him?"

"Come with me," he said to her, and he got up and went
across the room to the telephone. "How do I get information
up here? Help me, Martha." Martha got him the number. She
had to ask him to spell the name. She dialed for him. He saw

the twisted columns of the front door, then Billy Rea's apartment just down the hallway from the mailboxes. A voice answered, hurried.

"Hello, Billy? Is this Billy Rea? Yes, well this is Thomas Burden—you know? I'm up north here for the Fourth, but I've heard something about a fire—"

The voice barked back through static. "It's bad, Mr. Burden. Upper floor is pretty bad, part of the second. We thought you was a goner, too, until the wife remembered you said you was leaving."

"Was anyone hurt?" asked Thomas.

"That girl up there across from you, she's dead from the smoke. It started in her place, they think, and there wasn't nothing anybody could do to get to her in time. We had four trucks here, no, five. It's bad. You better stay up there where you are for a while, Mr. Burden. I don't know what you got to come home to. Just a minute, the wife wants to say something."

"Mr. Burden? This is Angie. Listen, your apartment looks just terrible. I know you live by yourself, and I want to tell you that I don't think you should come back alone. You're going to need a lot of help, hear? Everything's bad, I don't know what you've got left."

"Are you sure that girl is dead?" asked Thomas.

"She's dead, poor girl. One of the firemen he says to me he thinks she didn't even try to get out." Thomas heard himself gasp. "Now are you listening to me, Mr. Burden? You're not a young man. When you come back here, you got to have someone to help, you hear. Can you still hear me?"

"Yes, I hear you," said Thomas faintly.

"Are you done talking to Billy? The police is still here."

"Yes," said Thomas. "I have no more to say." He hung up. Martha had put an arm around him as he spoke. Now he was moaning, "Oh-oh-oh." He looked to Martha. "Did you imagine anything like this?"

"No, no, nothing like this. I thought she might go home to her family." She kept her arm firmly around his shoulders.

"If I had thought hard enough, I might have known," he said. "I might have known how to put everything together. Oh, I should have known something like this could happen."

"Will someone please tell me what did happen?" demanded Sarah.

Thomas came slowly back to the table. "You tell it, Martha. Please, you tell it."

"I think you should tell it, Dad." She stood behind him and began to knead his neck and shoulders.

"Tell them at least that she was out of her mind," said Thomas. "Wasn't she out of her mind?"

"Possibly she was," said Martha's voice above him. "But how were you to know that in the beginning?"

He leaned back into the ministering hands of his daughter. After what seemed like a long silence during which Otto scraped his chair back on the hearth and poked at the fire, Thomas began to talk.

"But wait a minute," interrupted Sarah after a minute or two, "what was the real beginning?"

Thomas closed his eyes. All he could hear was the fire and the breathing of four people and a short groan from the dog. "Help me," he said to Martha.

"You're doing all right."

He did the best he could. He did not attempt to spare himself. The telling seemed to be taking a long time, but after all was quickly over. "Someone else might see a different story," he said. "I can't make sense yet. I can't make any judgments." Both his hands lay open, on either side of his half-eaten breakfast.

"There's one thing at least that is clear to me," said Sarah almost immediately, "and that is that you must of course come home with Otto and me. Thomas, don't you see? Otto? Martha? Don't you see?"

"It does make sense, Thomas," said Otto. "I'd go along with that. Sarah and I have even talked about it before."

"No, no," said Thomas, "I couldn't possibly."

"You possibly could, and you will when you've had a chance to think about it," said Sarah.

"Really, Dad, think about it." Martha kept on rubbing his neck.

"Something would go wrong," said Thomas. "You'd be sorry you did it. You'd rue the day."

"It would please me. It might be good for all of us," said Sarah. "And where else would you go? No one wants to live in a hotel. Don't you see? This was meant to happen." Her cheeks had turned an amazing pink.

Thomas shook his head. "I don't see well enough. I don't know where you get your ideas. I have to think this through for myself."

"Yes, yes," said Sarah. "You think, but don't just *think*." She was looking at him intently. "We would be more than glad to have you with us—we *have* talked about it before, Otto and I."

In the centers of her eyes, beneath the blue, were tiny flecks of yellow he had almost forgotten about, like gold dust, or fool's gold, winking at the bottom of a stream. You had to look very closely to see them. You wanted to plunge in, hopeful.

Thomas straightened his posture. "I thank you, but if I accepted your kindness, believe me it would only be on a provisional basis."

Sarah touched his hand lightly, a questioning stroke. "Isn't everything?" she asked. "Don't you think so? . . . Thomas?"

"What can I say now, Sarah?" He searched through blue to the flecks of gold. "I will consider what you have said."

ON THE LATE BUS

Other people always stirred things up. Here was a fat man asking in a wheezy voice if the seat was taken, sweetheart, when Alison had barely gotten the sound of her stepmother's *Sorry it didn't work out* simmered down in her head, and so she had to cram her duffle under her feet on the filthy bus floor and allow this monstrous body to stuff itself down next to her, so close, just inches away. There was something wrong with the way buses were made. His breaths eddied around her. She heard him sucking, on a hard candy maybe. She was empty herself, no food. Going far? he wanted to know. What was *far?* Not speaking, she tilted her face toward the window and pressed her knees together, angled away from him. At least she had the window.

She was fifteen years old and nobody's sweetheart. The window was what she'd had for the last hour, and she'd used it to put golden aspens and red maples and dark green pines in the place of the people in her head, the ones who stirred things up the most—a father and stepmother in the place she was going from and a mother and her boyfriend in the place she was going toward. Sorry it didn't work out, said the woman in one place.

Who do you think you are! said her mother, the one who was supposed to know who her own daughter was, in the other place. Don't listen too much to your mother, said her father, she's what you might call disturbed. Cool it, said her mother's boyfriend. The evening light in the aspens was like a cloud of gold. Last night in bed—actually, a mattress on the floor of her father's small house—she had heard geese flying high overhead, the same direction her bus was going now, south, but for her that didn't make much difference because she was still riding straight into winter. The geese had sounded like geese and also like someone rubbing on window glass, far away.

The man had stopped sucking and was now peeling off the top of a package of gum. His arm poked out in front of her, too close, as he offered her a piece. She shook her head, no. She felt light-headed with hunger. Don't talk much, do you? said the man. He was unspeakable. She ducked her face. Fat people were disgusting to start with, and then when they did and said disgusting things, it could make you gag to be around them. She should vomit in his lap—that would cause a stir. She could be just as good a troublemaker as anyone else.

But the trouble was, she didn't have anything to throw up. She had refused her stepmother's cold cereal this morning and her sandwiches this noon—she wasn't going to take any more food from a woman who didn't even want her around. Finicky, she had been called, so all right finicky was what she was really, really going to be. Her stepmother had two new children, one a baby guzzling breast milk. Every time Alison turned around out came the bare breast again and there was another bald-headed half-brother getting exactly what he wanted and slurping while he was about it, too. The expression on her father's face as he watched was so silly it made Alison want to put a cooking pot or a grocery bag down over his head. The other kid always wanted her to get down on the floor and play with him, and the first few visits she had, until she finally figured out that this was just what her father and her stepmother wanted, to get her down on the floor and out of the way, and so this time she stayed stubbornly on their level, at the table, on the couch, her arms folded over her chest. Anyway, it was impossible for her to play like a kid, getting interested in whether or not the blocks were going to fall over, making the sounds of a truck—there was no way she was ever going to have that again.

What she did have was her eyes, good eyes, better than twenty-twenty, the doctor said. She wished she could go back to that doctor once a week and have him look at her and tell her about her eyes. Right now she could see so far into the trees that she could probably be a wild animal if she needed to. She could get off the bus and streak into the woods as her eyes were doing and never have to go back to one house or the other. Wild animal mothers sometimes took care of human babies. But she was too old for that. Anyway, what wild animal mother would want a child like her, an upright stick of a girl with ringworm on her left thigh and a coil of black feeling in her heart? She'd have to learn to *be* the wild animal, tough and wily, all on her own. Trouble was, in the woods she'd run out of that vile ointment she had to rub on the raised, scaly circle of the worm and then pretty soon her whole body would become one gigantic parasite. She'd be eaten up. Then she'd start infecting the whole forest. The other animals would run her out.

She caused trouble no matter where she was, even when she was absolutely still, her arms over her chest, just existing. Every time she came into a room where there were other people, in one house or the other, she could tell that she was stirring things up. No one knew what to do with her, even when she was doing nothing but breathing. One day her mother had fallen and torn a tendon in her ankle while Alison was walking right beside her, and just before her mother fell Alison had seen the split in the sidewalk—the concrete square was like a hardened country, she had thought swiftly, with something wrong in its middle—probably in time to warn her mother, clicking along beside her in her stupid high heels, and probably her mother knew that—that her daughter was to blame for the cast and the crutches and the difficulties every day in getting to work and making her way home and trying to stand up to cook dinner. Alison tried to help, but her mother didn't like her messing up the kitchen. Then, when she wandered into the living room to sit with her mother's boyfriend, her mother shouted at her for watching television when there was so much to be done. She was sent up to her father's so that at least the house would be quiet for the weekend.

At her father's she caused more trouble than she ever had before. Anyone could see that with the new baby there wasn't room for her now. This time they had put down a mattress for her behind a tacked-up sheet at the end of the bedroom hallway, under a tiny window. Well, at least she had had the window and heard the far-away, matter-of-fact music of the geese and seen the full moon, with its gigantic eyes looking back at her. *Sorry it didn't work out.* What did *it* mean? There was something wrong with the way sentences were put together.

It's going to get dark now, said the fat man, leaning toward her slightly and peering out the glass. Gets dark early now.

Oh boy, what a genius this guy was, a regular Sherlock Holmes. That's what her stepfather had called her the other day when she had said that college would probably cost too much. You're a regular Sherlock Holmes, Alison.

You goin' home or goin' away from home? asked the fat man.

Neither one, she couldn't stop herself from saying. Oh god, you open your mouth once and then there's no telling what will rush back to you.

Neither one? he said, breathing hard. Now that's a situation peculiar like mine. Me, I'm goin' from one daughter to t'other. Neither one wants their old pa. I bet you wouldn't do that to your old pa, would you? You're a nice, smooth-like girl. My girls, they've got pricklers all over them. He shook his head sadly. He sounded as if he talked to himself a lot.

What a creep! She wished she could give him her ringworm, that itchy, creeping circle that made her feel so dirty. She'd have to slide down her jeans and press her palm on the discolored patch and then find someplace to transfer it to him when he wasn't paying attention. She'd show him how smooth she was!

Her teachers used to think she was a good girl, before she started crossing her arms and not saying anything. She knew most of the answers, but what good did it do anymore to let people hear her? Besides, knowing an answer and keeping it to herself gave her a kind of invisible arrow that she could send out through her eyes toward the teacher, or anybody else she needed power against. The secret to being able to send the arrow, she was discovering, was not saying anything. She cast a sideways glance at the fat man, just with her eyes, and saw that his chin was lowered to his chest. Mr. No-neck. She'd save her arrow for when she really needed it.

Outside there were fewer pine trees, more coppery oaks, dying colors. And there were more signs of people and the messes they made. When she got back to the city, she'd be drinking softened water again and sleeping in the room right next to the giant legs of the electrical transformer tower. The water up north at her father's tasted like rocks. Her mother's boyfriend called the ice cubes in his whiskey glass rocks. He'd probably be the one to meet her bus, practically at midnight, and he'd be mad because her father hadn't come out of the woods with his chain saw in time to get her on the early bus. Her mother would be at home with her foot up, or maybe already asleep. The cast went nearly to her knee, and her toes sticking out of it were discolored.

The fall, the bad injury, the cast, the days and nights even more messed up than before—everything had happened so fast. One minute Alison had been walking beside her mother, being scolded and criticized by her and at the same time sort of day-dreaming about the broken sidewalk just ahead, and the next minute her mother was down on the ground, crying, Oh, my foot, my foot, and then every minute in their lives got more difficult. Like that, just like that mothers and fathers divorced—one day in the same house, the next day not. Earthquake, crack down the middle, fast.

And fast was how her best friend Lois had died last year, inside her white cast, from a greenstick fracture. Well, of course it hurts, you've broken it, just let it heal now, her parents kept saying, but Lois couldn't stop talking about how much her arm hurt. They took her back to the hospital too late. Alison had sat stiffly on the couch at her own house and heard her mother saying the words *gangrene* and *shock*. In the coffin at the funeral home Lois's honey-colored hair had been clipped back neatly with two barrettes, just the way she had always worn it to school. Don't get hysterical now, her mother had whispered behind her, but Alison wasn't about to let anything out her own lips. It was only in her room, with the door locked, that she would take out Lois's picture, prop it on the stem of her desk light, and let her own face crack open as she looked and looked at the smooth hair, the serene heavy brows, the sweet mouth that were now flat underground, facing up beneath the lid of the coffin. Fast, unfair—what could possibly be said? Lois was the last person she had laughed with, the real kind of laughter.

The trouble was with the people who were supposed to be parents. There was something so wrong about the parents that you couldn't even talk about it. Fast was how they wanted you out of their house, before their lives were worn out, before they had to admit the mistake they had made in having you. She had one other friend, Joann, who had been given exactly three more years to live at home. Graduation, and she had to be out the door, out, and that meant no more money, no food, no bed, no nothing, so she was supposed to start thinking now about what she could do ahead. Her mother had a new baby, too, and a new husband. Joann told Alison that having a high-school-age daughter around must remind her mother of how old she was. I could really give her gray hair if I wanted to, said Joann, but she's not worth it, I'm saving my energy.

The fat man was right: it was getting nearly dark. She should say to him, Hey, genius, look at that, you were right, it got dark. Pretty soon there wouldn't be much at all to see out the window. A wild animal at night, unless it was the night kind, crawled into its home with a full belly and went to sleep until daylight. Human beings didn't live like that. They traveled all night if they wanted to. They played around with what was normal. They turned everything inside out and upside down, they broke things in half, in thousands of pieces.

Close beside her the fat man took out a soiled handkerchief and blew his nose, loud enough to blow up the bus. Honk, blast. Alison closed her eyes. She felt faint with disgust, or was it just hunger? Her mouth tasted awful. She had never gone a whole day without a single thing to eat. Suddenly she thought, I don't know anything about life, I don't know any of the answers.

Are you one tired girl? The man's voice made her open her eyes. He didn't even wait for an answer—he had caught on to her fast—he just kept on talking. I'll tell you, I'm one tired old man. I don't have much left, and that's the truth. I don't know how it got to be this way, but it sure has.

There was that *it* again! Words sounded so queer to her tonight. Everything seemed put together in the strangest way, without enough reason. Maybe that's what happened to your head when you didn't eat. She thought about her duffle bag under the seat, no food in it, just her flannel pajamas and some extra jeans and her American history book. She saw that the fat man's hands were shaking a little as he clumsily folded his handkerchief and stuffed it back in the jacket of his cheap-looking suit coat. But he couldn't be shaking from hunger—oh no, he was too fat to be hungry.

Most people around the world didn't have much, she knew

that now. But for as long as she could remember her father had talked about wanting to be rich, the head of a big family—a sprawl of horses, dogs, buildings, pastures, children. Even these days he had schemes for getting the life he wanted, and he usually talked about someone or other who was going to help him. What he actually had now was a small house near a small woodlot, a chain saw, a stack of firewood, a job in a cannery, and a different family. If her father had been the one to offer her the sandwich at lunch, she might have taken it. But he hadn't even been in the house most of the day—he had been out in the lot making his saw scream through wood.

There was an acid-tasting heat in her throat. She wasn't going to cry! Not in this repulsive place!

I'd say we're going to have ourselves another moon tonight, like last night, said the man.

Well, what did he expect! That's what she could say to him —Hey, genius, what did you expect, it's like twenty-four hours later than the moon last night.

Then he leaned slightly toward her to peer out the window, and she was forced to see the side of his creased face, his jowls, his whiskers, his nose hair, his sad, red-rimmed, drooping eyes. He was a lot older than she had thought at first. Yes sir, it can be real pretty when it comes up like that, he said, wheezing, pursing his lips. For a while I thought maybe those clouds would keep it from us.

That's what he had meant, clouds. She hadn't understood him. She was sorry that she hadn't understood him. She looked as he pointed. The orange moon had just cleared the horizon. She didn't think she had ever seen it so close and so big. Last night she had had the moon whole, and tonight right here she had it again, even better. And so had this old man beside her, the one whose daughters didn't like him anymore. What could he have done to them? she wondered. Would she ever be like that some day—not wanting her father to visit? And where was this place she was going to live in, when she was old enough to have a father visiting her? And what was the way she was going to live, how was she going to be?

This tells me it's time to eat, said the man. He brought to his lap the vinyl bag that had been wedged between his feet. Mind if I do? he asked as he flipped on the little light over their seats. Now what do we have here? Well, ha, I ought to know, I packed it myself. Peanut butter and more peanut butter. Belle —she's the one daughter—didn't have much else to pick from. I would've liked a turkey sandwich, I could get my teeth into that. Now, what do you like, little miss? Are you going to help me eat these peanut butter sandwiches? I've got four. I thought, well, even if that's all she's got, I'd better take plenty. I learned a long time ago not to pass up a meal.

He lowered the bag to the floor, balancing the wrapped pile of sandwiches on his lap. Now, he said, do you want number one, two, three, or four?

None, she was going to say, I'm finicky, see, I don't eat much, though she would restrain herself from adding that she was especially finicky about whom she took food *from*, but at that very moment she was aghast to see her own hand snaking out like an animal's to grasp the top square package. Thank you, her voice said. It was what he had said about getting his teeth into a turkey sandwich that had gotten her own mouth so crazy for anything to put in it, she didn't care what kind of bread, or what was between it. And her stomach had grown hands that were grabbing and clawing for something to fill them.

That's better, said the man. It wouldn't do any good to have me sitting here eating in front of you. Though I've done that plenty, I'll have to say. Oh, he sighed as he bit into his own bread. It's not too bad. It'll do. You can turn that light off now, honey. You don't have to see to fill your mouth with what you've already got in your hands. Isn't that so? Oh, lordy, I always feel better when I'm eating.

She turned out the light and unwrapped her own sandwich. There was moonlight on her hands. She bit in. She had the moon to look at while she chewed, the watchful moon. Last night, tonight, this feeling of being seen was something new. She had a new secret, the strength of the moon, looking at her.

I'm not what you might think I am, said the old grandfather beside her. I've just been through some hard times. She turned and nodded at him.

This business about trouble, she thought. Everybody caused trouble or had troubles. And everyone lived off other people, in one way or another. She went back to chewing and staring at the cavernous eyes of the moon. There was something she was trying to get right in her head, a thought that had just appeared out of nowhere at the moment she had first bitten into the sandwich, something else about trouble, people stirring things up. Here it came again, from she didn't know where: if people could turn on the trouble, they could make other things happen, too, besides trouble. Was that what she had thought? Was that what could be called an idea of her own?

SMART BABY

Oh, it's so hot tonight! I suppose I should have said more to you on the telephone, but you were the one talking, as usual. What are you doing this minute? Opening your refrigerator? Ice cubes? Think juice, Leo, think water. I should have said, If you did it last summer, you can keep doing it. No alcohol.

Are you picturing me this minute? Probably not. Here I still sit by the telephone, stirred up with worry after your call, bare legs splayed in the heat, toes curled around the stair bannisters, and you're most likely already off in another part of your new house in your different city, old me in the old neighborhood forgotten again because you're still so busy with not liking yourself anywhere. Is it you I'm really worried about, or Bert on the road tonight, or Alan and Rae so far off in Africa, or of course the whole world . . . or just me?

Think lemonade, Leo. Cranberry juice. Think about me, why don't you. These are good legs, mine. Did you ever really notice them? Maybe not. Is the air as humid there? Here it must be about the same percent of water as another live body. Lots of women are alone in houses tonight, and the older they get the more they're alone. I know, I read articles. You called for Bert,

I could tell, but it was me you got, wasn't it? And I listened and listened. And now I've got you, on my mind along with everything else. I'm of an age where I should really be speaking this whole mind of mine, if I knew it—I mean, if not now . . .

I bet you'd be surprised if you knew how much Bert and I talk about you—yes, still do. I wish I could lie close to Bert this minute, drape a leg over his body, get him to remind me what it feels like not to be so churned up over other people's lives, which I probably can't do anything about anyway, which can't be a substitute for mine. Lady Bad Luck, you said tonight, she's the only one who has ever stayed by you. Why did I let your voice go on and on? I'm sick of what a good listener I am. I should have said, Aren't you forgetting an awful lot? I should at least have asked you please to remember last summer. You liked yourself well enough then to stop drinking—well, didn't you? And I would think our friendship with you would count for something. Wasn't this the picture: three human beings— four with Alan—but three of us older ones, more or less being witnesses for each other? Or were Bert and I just the ones chosen to keep an eye on you?

Sunset today was a relief. You told me one day last summer that funnily enough high noon in the sun, and not the evening hours of boozy memories, was when your demons could really buzz.

I study my legs, my feet. You'd probably mock me if I told you that this stairwell is a healing place, but you should see it tonight, so quiet and shadowy, with the light from one lamp glowing here and there in the wood. A hundred years ago pieces of oak were fitted together, piece after piece, and after a while there was this beautiful opening through which one could climb. It's like the spinal path of the house. When Alan's letters come, I read them here in this chair. Sometimes, with the letter open in my lap, I just close my eyes and let myself cry. The stairwell knows what to do with tears. My son and his girl, almost like my daughter now, are in another continent! On the map I carry in my mind, Africa is like a gigantic heart shape between oceans of blue. Every day I ask myself if it is still possible to do a mother's job—keep the children safe—simply by treading gently here, in this part of the earth, and trying to say what is true for me. I tell myself that small acts do add up to a world. Small acts . . . and self-knowledge—it's funny, even talking to myself, I can imagine your critical voice pronouncing with distaste the word *jejune*. But you yourself used to talk about getting sober as learning to go bare; even the great intellectual Leo had to grope around for a few inspirational words, to get by.

Leo, has it occurred to you that of the three of us last summer you may actually have been the most inspired? Anyway, what you were doing was one of the things that was happening right. You used to call yourself addled and rattled. Well, did you know how muddled a time it was for Bert, too, and how shaky I was myself? Maybe I do know myself a little better now. Last night, as I was falling asleep, I suddenly had a glimpse of my workable personality as almost separate from me, something useful just for a time, and I thought calmly, Oh, that's what it is—hello, you, *me*.

But last summer, even though I kept right on working and coming home and gardening and doing all my usual practical things, I had no such view. What I felt—and it was almost a physical perception—was that I was becoming sort of unwoven, with desperate questions at every fraying end. It was those ends, like groping tentacles, I started worrying about—I mean, what might I latch onto, what trouble might I cause? Rest was what I surely needed, maybe solitude, but I was working harder than ever just then, helping the admissions office to shift over to computers, being the right and the left hand of the new director, and in my free time digging in with the peace groups. The whole world felt frayed to me.

In addition, all that winter I had been reading so much about armaments, in the name of disarmament, that I had stockpiled more alarming facts than I could ever use in a lifetime of arguments. Even when I was alone, I could never tell when one statistic or another, or image of devastation, or recognition of complicity would fire off in my head. Joining the peace groups was my attempt to do something with those frazzled ends, the fears of destruction, but even that grass roots work—the long meetings, the newsletter, the telephone calls—wasn't doing the trick. I just didn't know what actions were effective anymore. I tried telling myself that this was just a stage I had to go through in order to change my thinking—come apart before I could weave myself back together.

Ashes of global destruction seemed to be mixed into my state of mind. Ashes could get mixed into the simplest ingredients, say the vegetables I sliced for dinner, which is to say that nothing at all seemed simple anymore. That's where you came in, inspired without even knowing it maybe. I'd be there at the sink, and I'd look up and see that you had walked through the back yards again to work in our garden—one of your ways, you said, of getting the poisons out, and a novelty because you had never picked up a hoe before. Ever since Karin had walked out, you had described yourself as being nearly in pieces, but from that distance I could see that you weren't as uncertainly assembled as you might feel. The form was holding, Leo! For Bert and me there wasn't much last summer that had the grace of simple rightness. But being your friend when you needed us seemed to. And being parents. And, usually, being our two selves together—though it's absurd how loving the one person closest to you can sometimes seem almost narrow when saving the world gets to be the focus. So I used to say to myself that for you and Alan to want to be around us, Bert and I must still have some broad goodness left in us useful to others.

Tonight I'm alone, but my head is so full of other people I feel as if I'm trying to give birth, as I have literally in my dreams now for month after month—I, the menopausal woman. When did I start having the dreams about the wonderful baby? It was sometime in the middle of last summer, when I wasn't even sure this person in motion was me, and then from inside came a miraculous dream child, born knowing worlds more than I, or so it seemed.

The dreams were even more miraculous last summer, given how overwhelmed I felt with the surface movement of life. In the flow of events—man-made or natural—so little was in my control. I had gone several months without a period, but I really didn't feel ready to stop menstruating. I needed to keep identifying in that way with all the seed-producing fruits and vegetables and with the young women I saw pushing their babies in the market. And some of my dreams, by contrast, were awful —where did they come from? In one of them, I remember, I watched from a high window as an unknown horseman in a flying cape cast an entire landscape into shadow as he galloped by—the field directly below me and beyond that a desolate finger of land, already a sort of no-man's-land, pointing out to sea. When I woke, my body ached as if I myself had been galloping all night. That man haunted me. He was like the opposite of the baby.

One night a woman I didn't know very well asked me at a peace meeting about my son, and I answered in the strangest way—not that Alan had just graduated from college and how much Bert and I loved all the joy and chaos of having him under the roof again and that he was talking of going off to Africa in the fall to study the figures and masks and that I had even painted his bedroom in the spring, which made it now the one room in the house that wasn't looking decidedly shabby—no, I didn't say any of these normal things. I said, He's always been a graceful child. And then my voice wavered and I had to stop talking. I left the meeting early and walked home through the dark heat, a night like this one, where I found Bert's large form

lank on the couch. One channel after another was flickering across the television screen to bursts of sound. It occurred
to me that there was something terribly depressing in seeing
a remote control in hands like Bert's, sculptor's hands, hands
I love, meant to touch everything directly, and he had started
watching way too much television lately, I thought. I strode
across the almost dark room and pressed the Master Power
button.

Hey, said Bert, what's the deal?

It's too much, I said. We're living wrong. Come to bed.

I left the room. I was exhausted. Behind me as I climbed the
stairs I heard the broadcast voices resume anyway. Didn't it do
any good for me to speak my mind? Our son might be inherit-
ing a world where grace no longer counted for anything, but
wasn't it still important that his father not spend night after
night in front of the television?

I filled the bathtub with water, dropped my clothes on the
floor, my underpants, and got in. Still no blood. Timothy threw
his seventeen pounds against the door and entered. He came
over and rubbed the sides of his mouth against the rim of the
tub, and then he rose up on his hind legs, draped his perfectly
striped front paws over the edge, rested his extravagantly whis-
kered muzzle, and began his ritual of watching me. I would like
to be worthy of the interest of this magnificent cat—not in
terms of vanity over my appearance, but in the way I am living
as a representative of my species. If I were a cat, what I think
would fascinate me most about humans would be their hands.

Leo, when I was listening to you tonight, I was trying to be
a good and helpful person. Oh, believe me, goodness was what
I thought I was about last summer, too. Live right and save the
world. But how much damage is done, do you think, under that
guise? That shocking incident with Karin let me know that I had
better hop to and take another look at myself, good Ruth—ha!
I have to shake my head now, just thinking about it.

What Karin did was to act out the bad girl in all of us, and

her banal adulterous drama also left me as the only woman—
and most likely more heady with righteousness and self-impor-
tance than I can admit even now—in the center of the lives of
three men. It pleased me that you had chosen our family when
you needed friends. Let Karin go and live out her mistakes, I
thought piously, let her think that discarding the past, leaving
two ruined marriages in her wake, could turn her into a woman
of the future. Here, I thought, here on the old home front is
where we're really learning how to salvage life. Maybe all those
horrible facts that I had taken into myself about *capabilities* for
annihilation—oh, poor, perverted language!—might be trans-
forming me into a charged woman, who was being given right
then and there a mission to become especially good at loving
men and at the same time capable of changing everything between the sexes, which was to say everything in the world.
Another instance of one-sided imagination? But you know, the
funny thing is that I can be at the far end of high-mindedness
when all at once I'll arrive at the exact opposite . . .

Anyway, there I was in the tepid water, a woman alone in a
bathtub. I tried to imagine what thread Bert could possibly be
following as he wandered between the channels. To most ob-
servers things must have looked fine for our family. Alan had
just graduated with honors, I had my nice job in the admissions
office, at which I was and am extremely good—well, my friend
Mandy Lifton, you know, the one I walk with in the early mornings, tells me that I should start giving myself credit for more
or less running the place—and Bert in the spring had won that
absolutely wonderful competition for the City Hall fountain installation, which to this day is the largest project he has had.

And, Leo, it's almost finished! Why didn't I at least urge you
tonight to come back for a visit? Oh, how your voice went on
and on about the human comedy, no laughing, and what you
called your genetic predisposition to failure—I wish I could
purge my head this minute.

Maybe what we call failure isn't so bad, for a time; it could be a chance for honesty. The trouble for us was that last summer our family looked successful, but things weren't what they seemed, except maybe with Alan. After the competition announcement, Bert had fallen into a terrible funk. I was so worried about him. I wonder how much you noticed. It was hard to say exactly what he was doing. He wasn't even teaching summer school because he had been given an advance to buy his materials and hire an apprentice, but June was almost over and nothing had happened. I don't know if he talked much about it with you because—well, *you* were our project for a while.

Bert seemed heavy to me then, dense with I didn't know what, whereas what I probably needed in my invaded state of mind was to put a few rocks in my pockets and do nothing but the most concrete things.

The bathtub: in a little while Bert came upstairs and slumped down on the floor beside it and said, What's the deal? without much spirit but at least not angrily. Being sullen with each other is not something we've ever gotten into the habit of, thank heavens. Timothy dropped to all fours and padded over to lie across Bert's legs.

There are places in the world where people don't watch television, I said.

What are you getting at? said Bert.

What if you were working on your installation instead?

It's ten-thirty at night, Ruthie.

I'm thinking about what went on today, I'm thinking about tomorrow, I said. I know how long you've been waiting for a chance like this.

Bert scratched the cat just the way Timothy likes it.

Finally he said, It's so big.

I listened—was he trying to be funny? Then I said, But you have the model. You won on that. The model is perfect. In my mind as I spoke I was seeing the model. I believed in it.

The model is small, said Bert.

I let myself just feel the water around me before I said, That's never been a problem for you before.

Bert leaned his head back against the white tiles. I don't know if I can do it, he said. I've been thinking that everything might fall apart once the scale gets that blown up.

What could I say? I knew he had even talked to an engineer about this one. The problem wasn't structural or probably even aesthetic. *You've got what it takes, honey?* That didn't seem like the best way to start changing how women and men talk to each other.

I heard Alan's car drive alongside the house to the garage. Close this door, will you? I said to Bert.

In our family we've never been particularly modest with each other, but ever since Alan went away to college and came home after intervals during which my own body had not been staying the same—well, I just felt like keeping myself covered, that's all. But Mandy's son did that frontal drawing of her right after her mastectomy, and she still insists that sitting for him was the best therapy she could have had. I probably never told you about that, either, Mandy's lopsided chest and sinewy neck and straight-ahead eyes and scraggly, new-grown hair drawn in charcoal. Why was I so reserved with you? Maybe I don't know how to have a male friend who is not my husband. I really wanted to bring more of myself forward for you to hear, maybe even for myself to know; I wanted you to like me and to look at me clearly. Instead, I got pretty good at talking in a way I thought would make you comfortable. Well, that's something I learned a long time ago; it's *my* genetic predisposition. Your occasional little fumes of scorn, of course, could silence me. But maybe even more oppressive were those moments when I would smell out your fundamental indifference.

I remember one afternoon when we were working in the garden together, you said that you felt your head was going to lift off from your shoulders, and I said, Funny, me too, and I can't even blame alcohol withdrawal. You didn't even ask me *why*. For a scholar you seem to me at times incredibly incurious. Or did you sense such weaknesses in my head that you didn't even want to risk venturing in? Was it that you needed me to keep on being a certain way? I more or less went right along with you, didn't I? Believe me, I'm so good at being the way people want me to be, even now, that I can make myself sick. Good old Ruthie. The perfect administrative assistant.

Tonight, when you spoke of failure, I did chance your mockery to remind you of Lear, stripped of everything and at last sublime, transformed, nothing left to lose except what could never be taken from him, but you said, Good try, Ruth, but no good—in this age a Lear would sink to his knees unremarked. And then I even dared, because at least you had said Good Try, to remind you of the power of love. How quaint of you, Ruth—is that what you really said? Well, I've heard you say it before.

One night last summer I said to you out of nowhere—no, not out of nowhere, out of *me,* the woman with the frayed ends groping for who knows what—you and I were making a salad, I remember, and Bert was in the living room watching a baseball game—I said that Bert and I had been faithful for all of our twenty-six years together. And you said your rather distracted How Quaint; I was trying to be agreeable as usual and so I said, Yes, we should probably be in a museum. But actually at that moment I was the addled and rattled one, not to mention inconsiderate, given your sexual predicament, and perhaps disingenuous, too, because you were looking very good to me, and, as I say, Bert was usually the one on the couch in front of the television, while you were often the one out in the garden or in the kitchen making a salad, with me. But I didn't *say* that I was addled and rattled and everything else. I kept on smoothly cutting vegetables! Quaint Ruth, who wants to love and save the world so much she has become a danger to everyone—was that the picture?

Maybe luckily for you your attention wasn't really on me. Whatever might have been racing about in my mysterious mental and physical circuitry must have been a world apart from what was unnerving you. I had put all the liquor out of sight in the high cabinet above the refrigerator—even you might have had to stand on something to reach it—but you knew of course where it was. When you were around, that cabinet took on power, as if some sort of entity were crouched behind the doors.

Anyway, there you were sitting at the kitchen table, heroically collecting yourself, I knew, for the task of being calm and making a salad, and I saw you eyeing the cabinet. And then you said, almost as if you were apologizing to that crouched Something—was it Lady Alcohol?—for a chivalric lapse, There's no harm in not doing what could be the death of you. And then at that moment Timothy leaped from the counter to the top of the refrigerator and sat there in his distinguished stripes and white waistcoat, directly between you and the whiskey, looking intently down at us, the humans. We laughed! I felt as if I had also been released from the grip of something not basically wanted. My head cleared a little. From the surprising turn of your words out of a string of negatives, I felt something shift inside me slightly, and for a moment, after months of cramped fear over the fate of the earth, I thought that the right changes could be easier than we had thought, for all of us. I was grateful to you. You grinned up wryly from the cutting board. Handsome man, and you were looking so much better without the alcohol! Oh, Leo, we had some good times, didn't we? Don't these count as successes?

Eleven o'clock, twelve where you are. I keep listening for Bert's car, but all I hear is my own head. I should have said to you tonight, plain and simple: You made a difference to us—

thank you. In that you were a success. I could have said just that, in a woman's voice.

Oh, that may have been the worst part of what you said tonight! What was it, so strange, and your voice a low rush, barely audible . . . something about being possessed, about having your power drained, all these years, by *women?* My god, Leo. You can do better than that! I'd rather live only in my own head than try to argue against such nonsense.

Those baby dreams, I think they began appearing about that night of the peace meeting, Bert and the television, the bathroom, no blood, the tepid water, the cat, my body alone, then Bert beside the tub, slumped on the floor. Without saying anything more about his project, he dumped the cat out of his lap and heaved himself up to close the bathroom door. Then he surprised me by taking off his clothes and joining me in the tub. He hadn't done that in a long time. He displaced about six inches of water, and there we were. Yes, that was the night, a shifting.

Bert said, Leo called while you were gone. He probably said this for at least two reasons—he didn't want me to bring up anything more about his sculpture, and talking about you was something that absorbed both of us, almost the way talking about Alan could. It seemed to give us energy, and, as I say, it made us feel as if we were good people.

How's Leo? I asked. At the sound of your name I was even more aware of our own bodies in the water, Bert's hairy grizzled one and mine with the two hills of puckered flesh rising on either side of the Caesarean scar.

Another clear day, said Bert, I marked the calendar—that makes thirty.

Remember the calendar, Leo?—how we had started writing the word *cheers* for you, day after day, and gradually for us, too, because we had also stopped drinking, in sympathy with you, but it was no big deal for us. I wished that calendar were keeping track of something larger: safety on the earth, no less, everything in balance, everywhere, no unnatural deaths today. But we weren't measuring anything more than one aspect of three adult lives.

Maybe we should consider opening a rehab center, I said to Bert. We finished washing, sprayed each other down, and got out. Music started up in Alan's room.

When I described Alan as graceful, I meant that he has always seemed to me poised, even as a child but especially in those months right after graduation, to go in any direction he might fancy—all he has to do, I think, is think it. I dote excessively on his talents, I admit, but I could tell that in those summer days he had gotten even you excited, too. You and Karin, in those few years we had known you both, had seemed to me rather superior in your display of childlessness, luxuriating in your travels, for instance, while Bert and I were pouring every cent we could into tuition. I never knew Karin well enough to question her about this choice, except I surmised that it had been choice, mostly hers, and that she had done whatever she had to do to insure it. Maybe she thought—and was right—that you'd never do your part in raising a child and that she didn't have the will to do it all by herself. But that summer with Karin gone and you on our porch with your mineral water and lime and a head stunned by temperance, you seemed to me more than academically interested in this exuberant messenger from the next generation.

I know we all loved the moment when Alan would shoot in the driveway from his housepainting job and pound up the steps of the back porch, where we'd be sitting behind the screens. For myself, now that the physical job of rearing him was so nearly done, I was reveling in motherhood. There he was, beautiful young man, even paint-speckled, and I had grown him in me! I might steal a look at you and Bert to see if you seemed to recognize my part in this wonderful person—the son to be enjoyed by all. That child, I thought freely, was definitely part of what was right about the world.

And having him home was gradually helping to ease the strangeness in my head. Sometimes when he wasn't in his room I'd just stand in the doorway, not touching anything except with my eyes, just wanting to think about his present life from that overview. I looked with an intentness I would have been embarrassed to use on him in person. I was thinking about him, but of course I was also thinking about myself, my body, my years, the quickness. And about nothing: I'd find myself just staring into the vacant space around the nodding pine boughs through his east window, on the other side of that sea of open bed and strewn clothes and sporting shoes and guitar and partly unpacked boxes of books, something I couldn't name, but that I felt as satisfying, from the vacant space . . .

Leo, nothing is failure unless you turn it into that! Tonight I also did hazard to mention to you your better self, and you said, My *better self*—the sneer came across the line!—has given up on me from too many unheeded messages. You dislike so much for me to use expressions like that. Once I made the mistake of calling a certain playwright great—Ibsen, I think—and I was submitted to another lecture, not on the lucky author, who, great or not, was beside your point, but on the schoolgirlish laxity of my enthusiasm.

Never mind: it's the baby I want to be thinking about, the wonderful baby who started entering the dreams. That night? I think it was. That night turned into something else, better.

Still damp from our baths, Bert and I made love, at first inside the sound of Alan's music—the lower tones, the beat, very primitive, was mostly what came through the closed doors—and then abruptly when the music was turned off we were at the center of the expanding night, near crickets, far sirens. Does it ever seem to you that bodies know much more than we know they know? Why do we all make so many complications between ourselves and happiness? That night, making love, I felt that there was nowhere else on earth I should be, nothing better I could be doing. Our movements felt large, Bert's and mine together. Why hadn't Karin been able to see that in wrapping arms, legs around one man, she could have loved everyone? It wasn't necessary for her to have exchanged one man for another!

I got up and went to the bathroom and drank a glass of water and brought a glass of water back to Bert, who when I entered the bedroom was raising both thick arms thoughtfully in the air over his face, turning them, studying them, pressing his hands together. He smiled at me and drank the water. Oh glory, I thought, oh holy living world, already perfect, in the middle of its flaws. We slept, with all the windows wide open.

Yes, and I had one of the new dreams.

I can almost feel it again: I am holding in my lap a beautiful healthy baby, a boy about five or six months old, just at the stage where he is beginning to sit up and look around. We are waiting for his mother to pump her breasts and leave a bottle of milk for him to drink later. I am sad because he is going to be left at a daycare center until night. He turns his head and looks up at me and says in a mature voice, Well, things are going along pretty much as usual. I am very surprised that he can talk.

I woke up astounded over the precocious, talking baby. I felt as if I were being instructed.

The first weeks that he was home after graduation, Alan had mostly slept and gone to work and come home and ate and talked on the telephone or with us on the porch and played a little music and slept again. Getting through those last months of college really must have worn him out. Then one Saturday he made his bed with fresh sheets, shoved his boxes under his bed and gathered up all his dirty clothes and started passing them through the washer and dryer in the basement. He tacked up the rest of his posters, mostly from museum shows, and some of his own life drawing studies and one of those marvelous ceramic masks he had begun making his last year at school. He shrouded his overhead light in a Mexican scarf and ran the vacuum cleaner quickly over the middle portion of his rug that was now uncovered. Then he made pesto in the blender from the basil growing by the back door and went with me to the grocery store where he picked out linguine and raspberries and bagels and cream cheese and all the other things he said Rae loved.

This Rachel was coming for four days. Bert and I had met her at graduation, under the trees, radiant under Alan's arm, and I think it registered with me that there was something very important going on between those two, but on graduation day there was a lot that was very important going on. And Africa was where Alan said he was headed, on the money from his grandfather and his summer job, and after that—well, he said one thing sort of had a way of turning into another—didn't I know? And I answered, One thing into another, nodding and repeating after him like a parrot because I was trying very hard not to interpose my stolidness between him and something I couldn't even see. He hadn't been talking that much about Rae, but after the first telephone bill of the summer arrived, I knew he hadn't been jabbering away with his old high school buddies. He had seen the bill on the kitchen table and offered to pay his part and I said, Well, maybe it's time, we'll see, but Bert said, You bet, pay up, and it was then that Alan had said she was coming for the Fourth, and then as an afterthought he asked if it was all right.

Bring her on, said Bert.

Are you going to give her a hard time then? asked Alan.

Absolutely, said Bert, scratching his beard. He said he would try to make her as uncomfortable as he possibly could.

Where will she sleep? I was asking before I could stop myself because I was picturing the awful mess in the spare room.

Do you know what I think? said Alan. You two are really a pair. That satyr over there with the beard is Saturday night. And you, Mom, what you stand for is Sunday morning.

When had our son learned to shift so deftly to an objective view of his parents? I could use some of that myself, I thought, that objectivity. It seemed to me passing strange that I could have gotten to the age of fifty without knowing very much about how to live.

Perfect! said Bert. You've got us.

I told both of them I wasn't sure I wanted the responsibility of being Sunday morning, and they both started laughing in my face. They told me it was written all over me. Except, said Bert—and he surprised me by getting up and coming all the way across the kitchen to put his arms around me—except I know she likes Saturday night, too. I'm the one who knows that.

You're going to like Rae, said Alan.

As it turned out, Rae was plainer and shorter than I had remembered from graduation, and I had a moment of dismay as I saw her walking beside Alan from the driveway toward the back steps. They're here, Bert, I said in a voice that didn't sound quite like my own. She stopped midway and pointed to the backyard with its wide rim of flowers and the vegetable patch. I saw Alan lean down to catch her words, felt a pinch in my heart, and thought, They're not matched! I hadn't known until that moment how preconceived my notion of a daughter-in-law must be. This young woman, if I held to my old ideas, I would never be able to describe as graceful. She was something else. I was still trying, probably too hard, to monitor my impressions when the screen door creaked open, and I was saying how happy I was to see her again, and Rae was shedding the backpack she had slung over one shoulder, and Bert was getting himself up out of the glider swing, and we were all shaking hands and clutching each other's arms, and I was very much aware that I hadn't changed out of my office clothes—plain linen skirt and

blouse and pantyhose for heaven's sake and jewelry and pumps!
Rae, straight from the airport, was wearing a sleeveless purple
T-shirt and a pair of loose, printed cotton trousers and some
soft cloth shoes. Her long brown hair was partly caught into a
high pony tail, and from her armpits hung brushes of the same
brown hair. It was Friday, five-thirty.

Somebody here is a wonderful gardener, said Rae sweetly.

Well, Leo, you're the one who may have found out first how
much Rae meant what she said, how sturdy she was, how she
wasn't just trying to be sweet. The next morning I woke up to
voices in the yard. Out in the garden there you were, with Rae
hoeing beside you, and by the time I was down in the kitchen
grinding the coffee, and Alan had come panting in from his
morning run, you and Rae were already friends, hot, both of
you smelling like tomato leaves and marigolds, and ready for
breakfast. You didn't often show up at our house in the morning, so I gathered that it must have been a fairly rocky night
for you. Bert had been reading late into the night, and when he
finally came downstairs he just stood squinting for a few minutes in the kitchen doorway at all of us, the scene. I felt awfully
tired myself; it seemed that all I did was just go from one job
to another, always busy and trying to have the right ideas and
do the right things, but after all was said and done I was just
one worn-out woman in the same old world.

Timothy had chosen Rae's lap right off, and he now sat upright, in bliss under her stroking hand. My head was having
another one of those days when it felt not quite part of me, and
it was mostly through her effect on intermediaries—you and
Alan and Tim the cat—that I was beginning to appreciate Rae.
Then I saw that she knew how to get on with Bert, too, with
her unaffected, matter-of-fact questions about his project, which
she must have heard about from Alan. It turned out that she
had worked in an uncle's foundry one summer. And the year
after that it had been a truck garden, where she had gotten

pretty good with her Spanish. A foundry and a truck garden! I saw you and Bert swivel more attentively in her direction. Who was this powerhouse of a girl? When I sat down to join all of you at the table, my body underneath my fragile head felt decidedly middle-aged, which of course it was, is. I tried sucking in my stomach, testing how far I'd have to go to reclaim my muscle tone.

Anyone looking at us from the outside would have thought that nothing much was happening. You appeared to drink your coffee gratefully. You had gotten through another night—have I ever really tried to picture how?—and so far you had kept your peace with the morning. Bert was raking back his hair and perking up to the sheer volume of life in the house. In talking to Rae about the casting methods he planned for his project, he actually sketched some shapes out for her on the grocery list pad—those abstract forms that we intimates knew were the soul of him, the fire and the water and the great earth body of the tree. Beside Rae, Alan had a vital stillness in his face, an intense, quiet pleasure. He loves her, I thought.

You spent most of that weekend at our house, except for nights—reading on the porch, cooking the salmon you brought over, talking with everyone. Karin had been gone three months. Look what she's missing, I'd think now and then, when I noticed a natural flush in your cheeks and a new steadiness in your voice. She hadn't even had the patience to imagine you sober! I was still angry at her, though I didn't realize how angry until she showed up later that summer. I just didn't know. I could see, though, even through the emotional clamor in my head, that one thing was indeed turning into another.

Later that morning I went up to Bert's and my bedroom, closed the door, and started trying on clothes, holding in my abdomen, in front of the long mirror on my closet door. Only Timothy was watching me from where he lay draped along the back rim of the easy chair, striped paws dangling on either side as if he were balanced on a tree branch. Silly cat, how could he be so fascinated with a middle-aged woman getting dressed and undressed over and over? I muttered to him about my appearance. I began casting away clothes. Once upon a time when I had been pregnant with Alan, I had had only three or four things to wear. I had held myself straight and gone for long walks alone. In carrying a child, I had been utilizing natural resources with economy, turning the right amount of good food into a new human being, focusing intensely, no matter what else I was doing, on the main thing.

I was taking perfect care of my child, then—would that there were something now to equal it. Tonight! I sit here alone in this homely stairwell, not knowing what actions might protect or help the people I love. Pray, my grandmother would say. Is my sort of praying prayer? I lie down on my back on the floor near the bottom step. This is the center of the house. I let myself become a corpse. And wouldn't you know it, here comes Timothy to sprawl across my middle and knead his paws into my solar plexus. I am trying to see the highway, Bert's car staying on course. Where is he, Tim? I say. Where is everyone? In Africa it is morning, morning light on their faces. This is the whole world. Timothy is purring; his eyes are closing. Who pictures us?

That first day of Rae's visit I felt so tired and ineffective, and lonely, in spite of the full house. I should probably just have taken a nap. What did cleaning out my closet have to do with saving the world? Pretty soon I had a pile of clothes set aside for Goodwill. Busy, busy. When I stepped out into the hallway, the door to Alan's room was closed. A little earlier I had heard you and Bert leaving for a tennis game. It was Saturday, the buzzing middle of the day. I carried bags of clothes directly out to the garage and set them beside the papers and bottles and cans that were accumulating for the recycling center, and then I rode my environmentally correct bicycle down toward the action center where I was to meet Mandy and Louise to work on the newsletter. The shade was too dim and the sun too bright, that's what I remember. The light was flashing off the angles of cars. I was speeding over bright places and darker, confusingly mottled places on the pavement. Then in a burst of light I fell. It's true what they say about the eternity inside an accident— first the recognition that it is going to be and then the slow, slow, motionless movement into it.

How did it happen? Bert wanted to know afterwards, and I didn't know what to say about where my mind had been. I should have seen the muffler pipe lying in the street, but I hadn't. I floated through an eternity and met up painfully with earth once more.

That night, while the rest of you did the cooking, I lay on the couch and listened to one of the Prokofiev string quartets I like so much. Being the bruised and road-burned one gave me a sort of temporary relief from trying so hard to live the right way. I got up and ate the good food that was put in front of me and then I turned my back on the cleaning up and limped again to the couch. This same noble Timothy jumped toward me, settled himself in the curve of my body, and commenced his famous purring. He breathed on me, worked his paws against my folded arms, narrowed his eyes as if he knew all about pleasure and everything else, too, and I was thinking that it might not be such a bad idea to give the world to this dignified, self-contained cat tonight, for safekeeping.

In a little while the four of you came into the living room for a card game—it turned out that Rae was great at poker, too. There was something impish about Rae, I thought from the couch, also grandly serious. There were voices and laughter from the card game, Alan's reggae turned low, and behind everything firecrackers from the kids in the street. You asked Alan what sort of music he was treating us to, and he told you, and then he said, It's the cutting edge, Leo. I was inside all of this. I started falling asleep, secure. It was wonderful. I was glad to have gotten knocked down from my insufferable posture. I was going to let go of the world for just a little while.

Later that night another miraculous baby dream appeared—I remember in the dream being surprised that my body has shed the pain of its injuries. In this dream I am holding a child who suddenly begins to nurse from me. I am surprised because I thought the child was too old and my milk was gone. My dress has special side-fastened flaps that easily open to my breasts. I am lying in the street feeding this child when a man stops to ask if I am in trouble and need help. I realize I must look very abject, but this is a facade. Underneath I am tough and capable. I tell him no, I don't need help, and I get up and stride away, no pain in my body, holding the child on my hip.

When I woke next day, though, I hurt plenty. Maybe the best thing to do for my soreness was to move around gently, I thought, so I went out to work in the gardens. You and Rae had pretty much weeded the vegetables, so I poked in the flower beds, transplanting some volunteer perennials, cutting back the early bloomers, mulching, thinking about what was happening to each of the clumps. You know, maybe just standing there looking and thinking is the best part of gardening. Pain was making me feel simpler that morning. It seemed to me that too much of my life had been lived in a cloud of fatigue and en- forced practicality. I looked back toward the house. *She* had lived there for seventeen years—Ruth, the daughter from the righteous, do-gooder parents, I myself, the one who still must have more to do—but *what* was becoming more and more the question. I resumed my work, moving gently.

From the direction of your house there hadn't been any stir- ring forth that morning. The dip where our yards abut was still in deep maple shade. I remembered how in previous summers seeing Karin sunbathing higher on the slope, perfectly groomed even in her bits of cloth and dark glasses, used to remind me that she was a travel agent, adept at knowing where else on earth it was possible to do what she was doing—we didn't know of course until later how temporarily she was deigning to lounge—in her own unkempt backyard. Yes, unkempt: the new owners, I must say, are devout trimmers, but compared to you, well, boring.

Leo, I do miss you! I should have told you that tonight, straight off. Could I have dared to say that in my regard you have always carried a core of light? Come on, Ruth, you would say, spare us the jargon. I was never able to tell you about those moments when you'd look up from something you were absorbed in, least self-conscious, and I'd think I was seeing straight through your fitful weaknesses to radiance.

I always found it odd how you and Karin never took a spit of interest in what was growing around you and then when she left it was not your yard but ours in which you chose to sweat out the toxins. Were there too many ghosts of memory over there? Lady Alcohol in the very grain of the woodwork? Lady Karin—where would you have felt her absent presence most? In bed would be the quickest to say, but where I picture her— though I never saw her there—is in the spare bedroom that she mentioned to me she had turned into her private dressing room, space for all her neatly tended clothes, plenty of mirrors, the ironing board perpetually set up, and a door that would close. How she must have picked her fastidious way through life with you! Touching selectively, is how I see her, gathering her skirts around her, secretly busy with contingency plans.

Oh, woe is me. I need Bert here to stem my acid thoughts. Tart. Two kinds of tartness, hers and mine. I need the satyr for a sweeter game. Are all women sisters? There are no personal solutions, that's what Mandy and I vowed together in the old days. I don't know what the old vows mean now, but I must have started to hate Karin for her bad faith.

When I went inside from the garden, I found that I had gotten my period, the last one, as it has turned out. I just looked at the blood for a minute or two, an old friend. Why, maybe I'll never go through menopause, I thought suddenly. Maybe it's not something that needs to happen! If I was going to change the world, I might as well change everything, all the old ideas. It was as fanciful a thought as the one I've had a few times since Alan and Rae have become attached, which goes something like this: I imagine that they have had a baby and have left it with me. They cannot return on time. The baby is howling, it is late at night. I do what is natural, bare my breast, tuck the baby in close and rub the nipple back and forth over his lips. He stops crying, he looks at me, he begins to suck. And lo and behold the milk is there, plenty of it, when it is needed, and I think, why not, stranger things have happened in this world than a grandmother with milk.

What is it with me this year, Tim-cat? I guess it's a case of babies on the brain.

I left the bathroom that day moving slowly. Alan and Rae were dancing in the front hall at the foot of the stairs—right here where I'm flat on my back now. Right here my son was dancing! He was really getting down into it, stomping, his hair falling over one eye. Rae twirled with her arms over her head. I noticed her waist. I thought, why this is going to be like having a daughter at last! I saw myself, twenty-two years old, the year I had promised to marry Bert. Dance with us! they said, and I limped in a clumsy rhythm through the hall and on up the stairs, but what was going on with them couldn't be entered by me, at least not in the state I was in. My job was to pause partway up the steps and look down on them and think what I hoped were thoughts toward a better life.

The weeks after Rae left, full-blown summer, Bert was really perking up. He went into his studio nearly every day, and as if in reward a suitable apprentice practically dropped from the skies. You, on the other hand, seemed to have lost your initial amusement with sobriety. It's extremely hard to go without a little something, you said, and I felt sympathetic toward you, respectful. That was the kind of plain, open-faced speech I liked, that drew me toward you. It was the other kind, bitter, snide, twisted, that I shrank from—because, well, it hurt.

One of those evenings on the porch I lowered my section of the newspaper and said something or other, and do you know what you said to me? You should have had more education, Ruth. Those were your exact words, insinuated into me before I had even thought to protect myself, and from your tone I heard that in your opinion it would never be possible for me to catch up. It was too late. I waited a decent interval, and then I put down the paper and took my stung feelings inside. It was at that moment that I probably felt closest to Karin. He deserves to be left to rot in his own juices, I thought to myself. He's supercilious and self-absorbed, and all he wants from me is dinner. He has no idea about what my life has been!

And I thought then and there, beside the stove, about my life: the upright, suffocating family I grew up in—tight-lipped with dislike of each other at home and in public desperate for the correct appearance, my early marriage, my job while Bert finished graduate school, my floundering about with motherhood, my jobs during most of Alan's school years, my catch-as-catch-can education, which you, of course, would never call an education, from women friends, from the world of men. At that moment I felt angry and cheated by everyone, starting with my parents, and on and on, right up to you with your cruel insistence on superiority. And Bert! Oh, I felt angry at him, too! How could he just sit there so ... so unaware? I felt like throwing the spoon into the pot and walking away. I was stirring blood soup. Was I just flattered to be in the midst of these men? What crumbs had I been living on!

But I kept on tending to the meal. Maybe my anger was poisoning the food—is that what you would think? The dangers of a woman. Ancient male fears. And my mother! Thinking about her was no help at all. What she would have said was that I was making too much of my emotions. Put on a better face and go out and help someone: that was her solution to everything. How ungrateful you are, she used to say to me— ungrateful for what I had been given, meaning, and starting with of course, life itself, from her, and a bed and food and work to do and a church to go to and on and on. I stirred the soup. I felt like a secret witch. Trying to put on a better face was what I had been doing all my life.

I served the food, evil me, who should have been speaking up, clearing the air, but, listen, try doing it sometime when no one else even knows the air needs clearing. We ate on the porch, in the beautiful evening light, but I felt too jammed up to feel myself bathed in it. Alan came home late from finishing a job; he was trying so hard to get money together for his trip. Everything's still warm, I said to him, Come be with us. I was glad he was home. But it was at that moment, while Alan was still in the kitchen, that the poisons—maybe mine!—really started working. You put down your fork. Bert kept on eating energetically. There was a pause. You still had your eyes on Bert. I stopped eating, this time like an animal alert for danger.

Look at Bert there, you said finally. Just look at him: he's got everything now, doesn't he? He's got the work, he's got the son, he's got the *girl*. Well, what d'you say, Bert, is there anything you haven't got? I bet you've even got plenty of clean shirts.

Girl? Did he mean *me?*

What's the deal? said Bert, looking up from his food. He really didn't seem aware how nasty the moment was. Hey, Leo, he said, is your nose still out of joint over that tennis game?

I was appalled, at the three of us. All along, unbeknownst to me, had we been trying to make you envious of our family? Had we been playing for our own benefit against your loneli-

ness? So much for self-knowledge! My head felt thoroughly gar-
bled. And I thought, This is it: the world is about to end from
simple ignorance.

Luckily, Alan came out to the porch with his tray of food,
and not a moment too soon. We talked of other things. Perhaps
that night was the beginning of the end of our mutual rehabili-
tation exercises. For myself, I was devastated by innuendo. As
soon as I could, I escaped from everyone and went upstairs and
took a shower and put on a clean nightgown and got in bed,
even though the daylight wasn't strictly finished. I did something Rae had told me about, massaging lotion into the feet at
bedtime to soothe trouble. It felt good. After that, I just lay still,
feeling my feet. I didn't even try to read. All I wanted was to
go to sleep.

How we hinder each other, that's what I couldn't accept as
normal. Above each person should be sky, plenty of room. A
strange image came to me, of a huge blanket thrown down over
all of us, under which we were struggling to move, humped
over, like one amorphous, lumpy creature, all of us held down,
struggling to stand up. Then my father's figure appeared in my
mind, the supposedly upright one, so proud, pillar of the community. I tried not to think of him, but I did anyway. I remembered how he had reported to me, long after I had considered
myself safely graduated from home, that he had once again had
the firmness of mind to vote against the admittance of women
into his business club, but I couldn't remember what I, his
daughter, one of those same women, had had the courage to
say to him in return. Was it too late to speak up? My father was
much older now, bent by his life, no longer attending business
meetings. I imagined him dead. I imagined myself standing up
straight beside his horizontal grave. I was shocked with myself.

Let me tell you, it was a relief to go to work that next week
and discover that I was still intelligent enough, educated enough
to be effective. Attitudes toward me from men twisted out of

their own lives, I told myself, and I wasn't obliged to accept hurt from them that had been given to them by others. It had to stop somewhere. So what was I doing—getting up on my high horse again? Heroic Ruth: the hurtfulness of the world was going to stop here with a woman who could take it, look at it, but not send it out again. Once again I was off on my mission, high speed, so busy.

Then came Karin, appearing out of the wide world for that shocking moment on our patch of local intensity, and in the middle of an August heat wave, too. Talk about buzzing! I learned later that she had come back to talk with you about the rest of your communal possessions because unbeknownst to us you were already casting about for other positions and thinking about putting your house on the market, but at the moment all I saw were her trim, tanned legs and delicate, high-heeled sandals, mincing across our property line, her white shorts, her slip of a blouse, her gleaming hair and red mouth, her jewelry. I was giving the new little rhododendrons a good soaking; I had looked out the bedroom window that scorching Saturday morning and seen with alarm their drooping leaves. I had the usual million things on my mind, too much to do in too little time, and the anxious sense that everything might fall apart anyway, no matter what I did. On came Karin trippity-trip toward me, skirting the mucky wheelbarrow of compost, wanting, I surmised, to coerce me by the force of her perfection into pleasantries and acceptance, as if everything were smooth again, as smooth and acceptable as she herself appeared. Surely I would be able to see by now that what she had done was the best in the long run for everyone—a new lease on life! But here's the thing: I saw her at that moment as holding the new lease and me as being one of those left to pay the bill. I felt like shouting obscenities, but I didn't say a word.

Are you aware of what happened next? I turned the garden hose full force on Lady Duplicity. Inside that moment of war-

fare I found another sort of eternity, for once I had started ru-
ining her appearance, I was spellbound into enjoying the
increase of devastation—the shocked then howling face, the
plastered hair, the sopping pretty clothes and pretty shoes. In
running from me, she lost her balance and fell across the wheelbarrow, which then tipped forward, sliding her and its contents
down, down. It was more than enough, but I didn't stop. I had
the perfect weapon, humiliating but nonlethal; besides, I was
now helping to sluice away the muck from the backs of her
legs. She flew screaming down our yard and up your overgrown
slope. Behind me I heard a screen door bang, and I thought, All
right, now I'll have all hell to pay, and the spankings of my
childhood, my father's spankings, flashed through me, but the
water just stopped gushing from the hose and then trickled to a
stop, and Bert came up from behind and removed the floppy
hose from my hand and let it fall to the ground, and then with
an arm very firmly around me he led me up the grass to the
porch and straight through the kitchen and into the entrance
hall where Alan and Rae had danced just weeks before and up
the afternoon stairs and down the same hallway that we walk
together after lovemaking, so molded by feeling that our entire
bodies can be softened into one continuous substance, and
through our bedroom door, which he closed behind us.

I tried to open my mouth, but actually I felt speechless, and
Bert must have been similarly struck—though perhaps I de-
tected suppressed laughter. What a wise man, I thought as he
began kissing me—why, I've done very well in marrying him,
we are truly a match for each other; if he can help to rescue me
from my worst self, maybe I can help him, maybe. Words did
come in time, but that afternoon a solution already seemed to
be appearing as our bodies moved.

Instead of being punished, I was being pressed more deeply
into the service of something else. Whether these acts I could
describe to you are small or large I don't know. When the bed

had stopped rocking, Timothy crept out from under it and leapt up to get closer to whatever it was we had been making between us. I'd like to think he approved. By the time we emerged from the bedroom, it was evening, Saturday night, our Saturday night, and the next morning was ours, too, to use as best we could. I felt as if we had gotten remarried, or as if both of us had come home after long, separate journeys.

For the rest of the summer, it seemed to me as if you were weaning yourself from us, and we, too, probably, from you. The real estate sign went up on your front lawn. Alan packed and left, just as the nights were turning cooler. Maybe someday I'll apologize to Karin. So far, I haven't seen her again. But I examine that incident now and then for instruction. I picture all of us as being in astronomical need of instruction. Who sees what we can be?

Now and then I still dream of the baby-who-knows. Isn't it strange: a woman at the climacteric with dreams like these? The baby usually comes in the very earliest change toward light, in the fissure between what feels like night and what feels like day. Just last week he appeared as a vigorously suckling newborn, who breaks off the suction to smile up at me with milk oozing from the corners of his mouth, and then he says in a deep voice that is both contemplative and sort of tough, *Good milk.* Oh! I exclaim. You can talk! Yeah, says the baby, philosopher, and pragmatist, again in that amazingly deep, world-wise voice, *I got words.*

Tim hears Bert's car before I do. He's off my chest in a flash. Oh glory, that's one more person safe, for one more night. I get myself up to the human standing position and follow Tim to the back porch. Some more aloof cats might not show how interested they are in our existence, but not Tim—he acts as if he's in it with us, all the way. Stooped over the trunk of the car in the lighted mouth of the garage, Bert looks like one of our ancestors, eons ago in the cave. In a minute he'll be up here beside me; we'll embrace. The yard all around is dense with various layers of darkness.

The nightmares still come, too, but they're less frightening now, somehow more familiar. I still sometimes see that original spit of land, the finger into the sea where the horseman rode. But the horseman is no longer there, just the abstract form of land, over and over, the same treeless shape, a bare extension, a digit with a wavery gleaming line along its shore, now pointing not away but toward me, as if I had myself changed positions and were in the sea of sky or in the water—as if I were the surrounding sky and water.

After I hear about Bert's trip, I'll remember to say, Oh, Leo called tonight—I talked to him for a while, but I think he really wanted to talk to you.

Leo? Bert will say. That rascal, has he ever been out of touch! So how's old Leo?

THE DEAD ALSO EAT

for Siri and Gillian

Day One

For me, this is just a job between one thing and another. Collecting tips, that's pretty good, nice quick fixes of money, but maybe what keeps me going even more is throwing words around with the other waitresses—anything funny that hits us, out it goes again, pong, like a ball in the air, like something wonderful that has to stay up there, moving, to save our lives.

We have special names for all kinds of things. The weird customers are "ghouls," and we probably get more than our share because of where we're located, between Mercy Hospital and the Greyhound station. Now this one in the corner booth with a plaid coat buttoned up to her neck for the last forty-five minutes, long straight greasy gray hair, black rubber boots even though it's summertime, eyes that look as if they're looking at something *I* don't see, she's definitely a ghoul.

She's all yours, Annie whispered to me when the zombie appeared in the door. It took her so long to get to the booth I thought she might be in a time zone the rest of us had never heard about. Then she sat so stiff, gaunt face without a smidgen of make-up, hands clasped tight in her lap, that I felt almost embarrassed about my own body being in motion as I went

over to take her order. Would she like something to drink? A
peek at the menu? My voice sounded loud and insincere to
me. I wanted to cover up my nose because she smelled so bad.
I'll have one Coney Island hot dog, she said in a low, over-
controlled voice, and then she looked at me in the strangest
way, as if I was supposed to understand secret meanings in her
order. But what do I know? I just slopped the chili on a fat
sausage, and that one Coney Dog is what she's been taking
teeny bites of for the last three quarters of an hour, sitting in
her ugly straight-jacket of a coat. She gives me the willies.

What else did you put on her Coney Dog? says Annie as
we're standing side by side at the soup station, loading bowls
onto trays, our tanned bare arms moving fast and saying to
anyone who knows how to add up details that for us this is just
a job between the beginning of our lives and what is going to
come next.

We get along great, Annie and Ellen and I. That week in
June when we all started working, it was as if we looked each
other over and right away made a secret pact that we weren't
going to let life hit the ground. Mildred says, You girls are a
stitch. Just in time, Mil! says Ellen. We all pretend to be in love
with Eddie, the dishwasher, and his stainless steel Hobart. Cool
machine, Eddie! we yell into the steam. Eddie is taking art
courses, Ellen is applying to law school, Annie dreams about
somehow getting to the Orient. She says she needs to get ori-
ented. I'm the only one who's living with a guy. It doesn't really
give me an edge or anything because I don't know any more
than anybody else what's going to come next.

When I get nervous about the future or bummed out by all
the crazy things that have happened, Jerry says to me, No hurry,
Nan, look to yourself, learn to live. That's what he has had to
do. Jerry's interest in being a psychologist doesn't come out of
being around normal people all his life.

But what still bums me out most, when I fall into brooding

on it too much, is that I thought learning to live was what your parents were supposed to help teach you. The big How To. Well, for both Jerry and me the facts about the parents aren't great: his dad deserted the family a long time ago, his mom is all mixed up over a string of men, my dad is a surgeon, but you'll never catch me getting near that knife, and my mom more or less killed herself. More or less? Jerry wanted to know when I finally had the guts to tell him about it during one of our early True Confession sessions. It was the first time in five years that I had used those words aloud to describe her car going into the tree at the bottom of the hill, one person dead—the mother person—no one else around, no alcohol, no heart attack, the brakes all right, daylight. The Accident, everyone called it. Sure, I told myself then, but very faint, way inside my head, so that I hardly heard it myself. Saying it aloud to Jerry, I could hear it. She escaped. Our life together, hers and my father's and mine, had been like a terrible drama, maybe even from day one, and then one day she just wasn't there anymore. No heart attack, but if you ask me, her heart had already been attacked.

But these days, instead of brooding too much on everything that was missing, I'm trying to develop this idea about circulation, about not holding onto anything too long, bad things or good. For the bad things I've made up a mental mirror that is supposed to zap them right back wherever they're coming from. I don't know if it works or not. With the good parts, like Jerry, I've got a theory that saying thank you—just in my head, recognizing them silently, but maybe sometimes out loud—might make them larger, by sort of giving them more energy. It doesn't hurt to try. Lately, I've been trying lots of the good things. If not now, when? I asked myself a couple of years ago, in the middle of college. I decided I didn't want to trash the rest of my life. Excellent decision, says Jerry.

The faster I move today, the more aware I am of how the witch in the corner booth isn't going anywhere. I'll be cutting

work to fill ketchup bottles and polish the milk machine before
she's done with her Coney Dog. This is weird: if I glance her
way, she's always staring straight ahead, away from me, yet it
still seems as if she's seeing everything I do. I don't like it when
someone starts doing a number on me. Well, what does she see
anyway? Twenty-three years old, skinny black pants and black
high-tops doing the old food service dance, grease spots and an
arc of chocolate malt on the polo shirt, pony tail getting frizzier
by the hour, plastic name tag that says *Betty*, which is luckily
not my name—nothing particular for a ghoul to get a hook into.
I think I'm safe.

I slide a bus pan of dirty dishes from the wait station and
escape toward Eddie and his Hobart in the kitchen. Eddie, my
love! I've got the ghoul to top them all, I tell him as I break
down my pan and load the glass try. She's a mutant.

Yeah? says Eddie. Does she have any messages for the rest
of us?

I'll have one Coney Island hot dog, I mimic in the ghoul's
repressed voice, imagining that my eyes look starved and secre-
tive. I know I'm turning into a good mimic; people often stop
what they're doing to pay attention to me. Now something
really gets into me, and I go on to describe the ghoul to Eddie
in an animated, derisive gush of words, which doesn't seem
exactly in my control. Finally I run out of steam.

Eddie says she sounds like a real character, and then he motions me closer to him and the scraping table. Look at this,
Nan—gorgeous, hey? For a close-up? He wants me to see the
multi-colored garbage spiraling down. Eddie's taking a course
in photography, and he knows I'm into it, too—a good camera
is one of the things I did manage to get out of my father. This
summer I've been thinking that somehow I want to make the
camera part of my future. And the theater, too, maybe—Mr.
Calder said I should go on; he said I could. Oh, I don't know,
I don't know. There are an awful lot of things to put together.

I take a minute or so to watch Eddie's beautiful, long-boned hands at work above the colors. If you've got time to lean, you've got time to clean, that's what the manager would say if he were here, but he's not, just Mildred and her husband Jack in the kitchen, and they're human.

Another part of my theory of circulation is that you can get and give energy just from concentrating on something that intrigues you—out the attention goes, then around and back, over and over. *Something* is generated.

It doesn't seem as if I'm leaning more than a minute or two, watching my attention go out into Eddie's hands and return to me, but when I go out to the floor again, the ghoul is gone, vanished. I don't rush over to clear her table and check for a tip because older women often stiff you—maybe because they've been stiffed so much themselves—and this particular one— well, forget it. I refill some coffee cups, take a few more orders, wipe up the drips around the soup vats. Mildred slides plates under the warming lights and calls, Order up, one-sixteen! That's me, *Betty.* Yuck, meat loaf and gravy, brown on brown. When I get home, I always smell like grease, my hair, my clothes, even my high tops. I usually go straight for the shower. I would rather have worked at the Stone Soup, the vegetable paradise below Jerry's and my little apartment, but they didn't have any openings this summer.

Actually, both Jerry and I have jobs out of sync with our principles: here I am, serving up dead animals and gravy, and he loads bags of ugly compound into the briquet hopper at a factory that turns out plastic handles for cooking pans. The compound that is digested by the hopper Jerry calls "mean dust balls," and he calls the briquets that are shit out "evil cookies." But there are two good things about his job, he says: the mechanical force-feeding of the die knocks out a sound that can be turned into industrial rhythm and blues—ba *doo* ba da, ba *doo* ba da, which he simulates for me when we're doing dishes, fast—and the open-web steel joists over the compound bags in the warehouse are great for taking a few Tarzan swings when he's a bag or two ahead at the hopper—his muscles are getting to be something wonderful. I come home smelling of grease, while he reeks of phenolic compound. Sweet couple. But he's making pretty good money for graduate school in the fall. And me? Well, tune in again six months from now, folks—a lot could happen. We're not stuck anywhere, though Jerry and I talk all the time about how working too long out of sync with yourself is no laughing matter.

I'm still avoiding the ghoul's booth. I clear a table where a little kid was, stack the booster seat by the wait station, get the broom and pan, sweep up about two cups of food from under where the kid was sitting. Cute little kid, though. Some day, I don't know, maybe I'll have the guts to raise a kid. First, I've got to raise me.

As long as I'm sweeping, I take a few swipes under another table, then under the ghoul's booth, and then with the long handles of the broom and dust pan in one hand I reach for a couple of her dishes—maybe I can balance everything—and then I see, right beside the ash tray where a lot of people tend to leave tips, a tooth. A very small tooth, not the adult variety. A milk tooth—isn't that what they're called? The Tooth Fairy kind. It has a little ridge of dried blood at the root end. I don't touch it at first, and then I see some new people coming toward the booth, and so I plink it onto the Coney Dog plate, flash the people a false and radiant smile and tell them I'll be right back to wipe their table, and then I travel at a very high speed over to Annie at the wait station. Oh my god, Annie, will you look at what the ghoul left? I hiss, but neither of us knows what to make of it, and there isn't time to do much more than gasp and clatter the plate with the tooth into the bus pan—a pearl for Eddie.

Day Two

Rain today, so the turnover is slow. That guy who's trying to fix his Walkman with a table knife has gone over three times to the wait station to fill his own coffee cup—I can never get to his empties soon enough. When I asked him earlier if he wanted some food, he answered—almost shouting because he was still wearing his Walkman then—Why would I want to order food when I can get it free at the church! The people at surrounding tables swiveled to look, and all of a sudden I felt as if I'd really done something wrong. I went for deadpan rather than the histrionic grin.

It's hard for me to tell how old some people are. Little kids, people my age, and the real fossils, those are easy enough, but in between are four, five, six decades of indefinite territory. Ellen's parents are here for lunch today, which they do occasionally because they both work as technicians at the hospital. They recognize Annie and me now, too, so we usually go over to joke with them and tell them all the things they shouldn't order, like the fermented apple salad and the Turkey Salmonelli. Ellen calls them the parental units, or "rentals" for short. I like that —I mean, parents aren't permanent, even pretty good ones like Ellen's; it's not as if you own them—or as if they own you.

But if there's no owning, then why does it feel as if there's disowning? Now there's a trouble nub. Don't brood, I tell myself, don't dwell.

I'm kind of jumpy today. I haven't been jammed up like this with my old nervousness for months and months. Actually, I've had some just great days lately where I'm happy for no particular reason, my eyes feel calm as I'm looking at the world, my whole body is calm, nothing spills at work, I don't bump into anybody, the bus is practically waiting for me at the curb afterwards, or maybe Jerry and I get ourselves into the invincible funny mode, like last Sunday, flying the kite on the beach, where there was nothing we couldn't turn into laughter. But today I feel locked in and jammed up, and I'm thinking about everything all at once but nothing clearly. Maybe it's just because I'm not sleeping so well this week, with Jerry on swing shift. Anyway, I'm a mess.

Ellen's parents leave her a ten-dollar tip folded inside a piece of paper with cartoon faces of themselves drawn on it. She shows the drawings to all of us, Eddie too, around the corner in the kitchen. If my father lived in this city, first of all, he'd probably never come here for lunch, no matter who his waitress was to be, and second, he'd never do a beautiful silly thing like leaving a hundred per cent tip. He'd leave ten per cent, maybe twelve on the outside, or maybe nothing, on the theory that children who are my age should stop expecting anything from their parents. He'd be trying to put me in my place, opposite his freedom.

Awesome, says Eddie as he hands the piece of paper back to Ellen, who has stuck the ten-dollar bill upright in full view in the pocket of her blouse. Seed money, she says as she gives it a satisfied pat.

I'm feeling really edgy as I head back out to the floor. For about a minute I'm thinking that I'd just like to fly out of my place in life, my upbringing, and try for a more satisfying one, and then I remember Sunday afternoon, running on the beach with Jerry, holding to the kite for dear life, and how I thought I might never have been so happy. I don't want to give up my past if it means I might have to give up my present, too. The tensile pull in the strings sent something tremendous down my arms as the air sucked the kite up, like an infusion straight into my center, which was a fantastic example of circulation of energy, and all the while as I watched the kite up there in the currents of air, everything down below, where we still were, sort of evened out and seemed livable. They're umbilical cords! I shouted through the wind to Jerry, and we were both laughing and high from the wind and the way the sun was hitting the kite and us, and all the way home we were still laughing and laughing and kidding around about billy cords and belly buttons, and then when we were kissing later I felt everything smooth out around us again, and he was like a root coming to me from the sky, and I called him Billy, still laughing, Bill. This could be the beginning of heaven, I thought, it really could, and I remembered to say thank you in my head, thank you, and then I actually said it aloud, to him. Thank you, and he said, surprised, Any time!

But today I can't get my magic mirrors set up against the bad stuff. I'm exhausted. Coming out the passageway from the kitchen, I bump my shoulder on the corner of the milk machine, as if I'm clueless even about how much space I need to move around in. I wish I could just cut work early and go home and pull the bedcovers over my head and be in the cave with Jerry for a while. Maybe we're not steady enough for this crazy swing shift schedule—maybe nobody is. I've lost all my starch today, I think, and then I feel even stranger because *starch* is not how I talk to myself; it's how my mother used to talk. I stop for a second on the edge of the action to try and get a grip on which one of a hundred things I should do next.

Then I see her. Like a shadow against the rainy window, in the same corner booth, faced rigidly in the same direction . . . is the ghoul. I nab Annie as she steers around me. You take the corner booth, Annie, please. She glances toward it, and then she says, No way! I'm taking the punks with the smoke and the onion rings for you, so you inherit the ghoul. It's true: I begged out of the smoking section because I didn't have the stomach today for those surly kids with purple hair and safety pins in their noses and nonstop cigarettes. If I had as much nicotine and caffeine in me as they have, not to mention greasy onion rings, I'd be totally out of control, probably careening around making zooming zipping noises like the aerobat. As it is, my heart is racing.

I do a few other things to stall for time before I go over for the ghoul's order. I plan to adopt a bored monotone, but when I actually start to speak I feel as if there's a clamp around my throat, and what comes out is a choked whisper. Watch her, folks, the future great actress in the middle of a nightmare: no voice, no preparation. This is life. But the ghoul hardly seems to know I'm talking; she knows what she wants from me, and she uses the same words as yesterday and gives me the same supersignificant look, as if I'm supposed to creep right off to a corner and decode the words *Coney Island hot dog*.

I try to tell myself that my reaction is out of proportion to what *is*: she's just an unfortunate, disturbed person in inappropriate clothes trying to act normal enough to get some food into her. I've got to be gentle with her the way I am with the four Downs syndrome people who come in regularly and order exactly one cookie each and two decafs and two regulars. Everyone, I tell myself, has a right to sit inside out of the rain and eat a little lunch.

But I don't feel gentle or steady as I load the hot dog with chili and cheese and onion. I'm revolted by the smell of it. Her presence over there in one of *my* booths seems shockingly out-of-bounds. I'm disgusted by her dismal coat and her boots and her dirty hair, appalled that she is ordering something from *me*, this turd and lumpy red spew on a bun. Why is she by herself? Why doesn't she have a friend? Why can't she make life seem less awful?

I set the plate in front of her, refill her water glass, and walk rudely away without a word. This is a rude, unstable world, I think, and there's no way to make it otherwise.

Hey! shouts a man's voice as I pass between tables. When are you going to call me? Hey, you, with the curly tail! *What?* I say, spinning around like the aerobat in a change of wind, and there's outrage in my voice, genuine, but he can't hear me because he has his earphones clamped back on. And his coffee cup is empty again, and me without a pot. Everyone is looking at us. Call me tonight, Betty! he shouts. I mean it, call me tonight!

Did I ever really think I wanted to be on stage? I was crazy. This is no fun, and this is not funny. I'm not at all myself. I don't know who I am. I walk straight off the floor, down the passageway, into the kitchen, through the metal doors into the walk-in cooler. I tell myself I'm going to get some cream, a normal thing for a waitress to be doing. I stand inside the cooler and close my eyes and listen to the cooler fan and smell the milky, cheesy cold. When I come out, my hands are empty. I'm shaking.

I go out to find Annie. You've got to take that booth with the ghoul, I tell her—you've got to. Just give her this check when she's done and clear for me, please, Annie, please please? I'll restock all your condiments later, I'll even condense your mustard, I'll do anything, please, Annie.

This is extremely strange, says Annie, but she gives me the loaded bus pan she's holding, in exchange for the ghoul's check. You still owe me one, she says.

At that moment the smokey zone of the punks where I'm standing seems like a haven. I love them for the protective haze they're blowing out, for their black, studded shells of leather and wonderful chains and flagrant hair, and for their fierce, mocking voices. I'd like to slide in between them, disappear inside the black and purple and metal and smoke. Security guards! Brothers and sisters! It hits me all over again what a loss it has been not having had brothers or sisters—all those years of no one else knowing what my parents were really like. Even these days, telling Jerry, I can't give him the inside view; the chance for that is gone. The chance for my childhood is gone.

I unload Annie's bus pan and stack the glasses in the Hobart tray, but I can't think of a single funny thing to say to Eddie. This is awful; I'm losing my sense of humor *and* turning into a paranoid.

Still raining out there? asks Eddie. He doesn't sound like a genius himself. Maybe this is the day life hits the ground, maybe it will never get up again, maybe we've unloaded so many bus pans that we've ruined our talents forever.

Yeah, I tell him, it's still coming down.

I take some more orders, make a few malts, restock the bean and bacon soup vat, wipe here, wipe there—all the time not looking at the ghoul and yet knowing exactly how she's eating her Coney Dog millimeter by millimeter. I'm so tired I feel as if my juices are being sucked out, just enough left to fluster my heart and jam up my throat. Jerry might still be lounging in bed with the newspapers or one of his psychology books. I'd give anything to be there with him, reading or playing, natural again, the window open to the good smells of the rain and the Stone Soup, music on maybe, energy circulating. My legs, I have no strength today in my legs.

Up the stairs I'd have to go with her breakfast tray, down the hall, into the terrible room where she had spent the night, where I, awake in my own room, had had to hear her spending the night. I was seven, I was ten, I was twelve; the years were going by and I was making the breakfast for both my father and mother, making my legs go up and up the stairs, down the hall, toward I never knew what. I would hear my father's car pulling out of the drive on his way to do rounds at the hospital; he would not be there to help me with whatever degree of disturbance I would find behind the door of her room. Judgments? Cold silence? Fury? I've tried to tell Jerry the feeling of that moment, when, dressed in my school clothes as a kind of armor, holding the tray, I would push open the door with the side of my body, my eyes trying to adjust to the dimness inside, my heart pounding, my skinlessness willy-nilly exposed.

I rise up from a crouched position and hit the top of my head on the open metal door of the salad cooler, so hard I want to be a baby with the pain, and I'm incredibly frustrated because I did it to myself as usual, left the door open, tried to do a series of things too fast, out of order. I shut the door hard. I'd like to break it for hurting me. I've got tears in my eyes now, I'm snuffling; this is no act.

Okay, says Annie's voice behind me, I've done the job, but you get the prize, tee hee. Her hand reaches around me and slides something other than coins into the pocket of my apron. No fair! I say, but Annie gets away. I squint over my shoulder to the corner booth; the ghoul is gone. When my hands are done with the mayo, I wipe them and reach into the pocket. This is not something I want to be doing. What I pull out is a sort of chain, made of safety pins of all things, hundreds of them, large and small, some rusty, some shiny, but not clipped simply together end to end—oh no; each of these babies is strung with five, eight, ten other pins, some of which in turn are strung with others, like caught fish dangling every which way, some nice, some not so nice, before being attached to the main circle. It is a circle. It's a crazy necklace. Who would take the time to make a useless thing like this? I'm almost fascinated. I can see taking this home to Jerry, watching him goof around with it, make up theories; maybe we'd end up hanging it somewhere, say from one of the light pulls. Hey, heavy metal—that would be Jerry's voice. I hold the necklace out at arm's length, almost fascinated, and then I look over and see Annie laughing at me from the milk machine. I've been had. I scoot over to her before she's done filling her glasses.

No fair! I say. You're playing a joke on me.

No joke, that's your tip from the ghoul.

It's not mine. You gave her the check, you've got to take it, I say. Anyway, you're tricking me—she can't have left this.

She did, and it's all yours, says Annie, laughing some more. Be creative, she says, and then she sails away from me with her tray of milk. I'm left standing there by the stainless steel machine with its plastic nozzles, holding a necklace made of scavenged safety pins.

The necklace is bunched up in my hand, almost the feel, but

about ten times too bulky, of the chains I used to throw for hopscotch in the schoolyard. Sudden laughter from the smoking section shoots into me like adrenalin. Okay, I tell myself, just keep moving; maybe the magic mirrors aren't working, but you still don't have to hold on to anything. Circulation, circulation. Am I calm and clear-headed? What a laugh, but I'm moving— look at her, fans, and she's on the edge of inspiration.

Okay, here she goes, sashaying over to the punks, easy does it. All nerves, she's about to play the scene. She stacks up a couple of their onion ring baskets, easy, laid-back, Betty-on-the-job, and then she says, no excitement, Saw something in the Lost and Found I thought you guys could use, and she drops the hot merchandise in the center of their table.

Hey, wild! one of them says.

They're a little younger than I am, just kids, my little brothers and sisters.

You want to give this *up?* another one asks.

It's all yours, Betty tells them. Be creative.

And then I'm gone.

Day Three

This is it, today I'm really going to try and do everything right, not lose my cool. I've even had the cleverness to ask for the smoking section, just in case you-know-who comes in to her favorite booth again. Watch me: mellow, smooth on the surface; forget that my head feels as if it's full of chittering squirrels.

Is your ice cream yummy? I gush to one of the booster seat kids. I'm the angel waitress. I'd like to rescue this baby from crude parents who sit there blowing smoke all around her. Well, at least there are two parents, that's one good thing. The little kid opens her mouth to grin at me, and more ice cream oozes out. There's ice cream on the table, on the booster seat, every-where.

It's hot today, steamed up after the rain, but me—am I going to get steamed up? No, angels just float around, soft and cool like cotton. I grin back—yet who is this one-who-grins? Jerry was asleep when I left this morning, and I was asleep when he got home last night. Without our daily talking and kissing together, I'm even more aware of the weird music of my random inside life. Somehow, I've got to learn to dance with myself.

A shaggy bear of a man sat down a minute or so ago; now his head is bent forward, huge back and shoulders sloped. What would it be like to dance with this guy, I wonder, dance with a bear?

Hello! I sing out. I'm Betty and I'll be your waitress.

What are your specials? he asks. He's sloped over a menu.

I tell him about the Turkey Italiano and the Western Burger. I reach in close to point to the Specials card attached to the menu. Or do you see anything else you'd like? I ask.

Well, what is there? he says.

Okay, I say to myself, cool it, maybe bears don't read. I tell him about a few other items, the cashew chicken, the fruit salad. Here and here, I say, and I point to the menu again. Maybe this is the day he turns literate, I think. I'm the cheerful angel, cotton wings covering her own wild inside sounds, who teaches bears to read.

Do you have any soup? he asks.

Sure, I say, and I point to the list of soups and the soup du jour on the Specials card. Chicken chili, I say slowly, pointing to the two c's, and emphasizing the sound.

Suddenly his head swings up and he says in a loud, critical voice, too loud for just me, I'm a *blind* person!

My own eyes shut for an instant, and I hear the squirrels going crazy inside, telling me I might as well forget the mellowness act, the no mistakes, because I've already blown it. The angel fails again. Here's guilt once more, jabbering away.

I'm sorry, I say, I didn't know, I'm *sorry*.

The man is still hunched over his menu as if it were a flotation cushion. This isn't my fault! I think. How could I have known he's blind when he's holding onto a menu? I list all the soups for him, I read almost the whole menu aloud.

I'll have some iced tea, he says.

Iced tea, I enunciate, writing on my order pad. I'm careful not to say anything more.

Plenty of sugar, he says.

Coming right up, I say, tea, plenty of sugar.

I want the tea *iced,* he says.

Yes, I say, iced tea with plenty of sugar. Finally he nods and seems as satisfied as maybe he ever gets.

Oh lord, I think, and I head off to mix what I hope will be the most unproblematic glass of tea in the world.

In high school sometimes I felt as if I might be able to make everything all right. During the day in my classes I would rehearse a behavior plan that might work when I got home, something I could say or cook, music I could play to make the house happier. Many, many things were problematic for my mother: her head, her body, my father, the house, the town, and, of course, me. *She was never the same after you were born,* my father said to me once, and his sister, formidable Aunt Barbara, concurred. I had created chaos. They were sitting in the kitchen after one of my mother's attacks—attacks on everybody, that is—and I was putting the food from lunch into the refrigerator; I remember exactly the doubleness of feeling a mechanical cold along the front of my body and an emotional heat on my back, where they both must have been looking. Freeze that pose and ask, for the record: how could the kid have made herself unborn? What I was learning was that being watched doesn't begin to make up for not being watched *over.*

Your tea, I say to the bear as I set the glass in front of him. Would you like me to add the sugar?

He nods. I want a lot of sugar.

Why, he's just an overgrown cub, I think, softening a little.

All right, I say, I'm going to put a lot of sugar in your glass of tea. I pour and mix and pour some more. Who are the genuine big ones around here, I wonder. Who are the ones large enough to watch over and contain everything? Me, I'm just a baby, too; it's a miracle I can manage to put sugar in this guy's tea. That should about do it, I say to him.

I've been so absorbed, like a workhorse with blinders, in trying to keep the hulking baby bear from being mad at me again, that when my peripheral vision returns I realize I'm way behind in my work. I go into high gear; I guess I'm still trying to do things right. The punks came in behind my back, and now they're clamoring for service.

Hey, Betty! One of them stands up, opens his leather jacket, swells his chest. Check this out—what d'you say, huh, Betty?

On him the safety pin necklace looks like a string of amulets hung protectively by the wise mother crone of punks. Or the big sister: that would be me. It looks perfect, I say. And it does. I feel a sort of aesthetic satisfaction as I take their order: a very strange piece of the world came to me, and I sent it out again in an almost magically pleasing way. I would rather it hadn't come from a ghoul, but, well, there's nothing I can do to change that.

What's important is that my theory of circulation might actually work. There's more in the head than squirrels! Then I say to myself, Okay, okay, don't swell yourself up, calmness is what you're looking for, remember maybe you're actually learning something here.

Onion rings, coffee, I write in my pad.

Hey, Betty, says another one of the punk kids, can't you find us any more good stuff like that?

I'll do my best, I say, and maybe I really do start to feel serene as I head off toward Mildred with their order.

But then my legs go weak, and the squirrels switch to strictly foreign languages.

She's there, uncanny, undeniable, not at her usual booth on

the nonsmoking side of the planter, but at a little table next to a column in the section I so cleverly maneuvered today for my own protection, from her, and I don't even have time to find my breath because she's actually beckoning me toward her, and my mind has leapt five hundred miles and fifteen years to the butterflies a neighbor boy gassed in jars for his collection, in that other time that really must have happened, childhood, just across the alley of hot blanched light between our houses, inside the dark opening of his family's garage.

Same plaid coat, same rubber boots, same stiff posture, same monotonous yet charged look in her eyes, same intensely delivered food order: she's stuck. If I could breathe, I would scream at her—anything to change her, or to say no, No food! But I have no voice. It's as if all my inside jitters are right there in front of me, glaring back and possessing me all over again, choking me—I can't get separate, disown anything. I write down *Coney Dog*.

Like an automaton, I stay in motion for the next half hour, fill her order, try to fill the wishes of everyone around me. It's a miracle my legs are able to do their job. Even the floor under me feels unsteady, the most uncomfortable stage in the world. No matter what I'm doing, I feel followed, and I'm too alone, too alone, I don't know if I can keep going.

Finally I get caught up enough to escape for a minute to the kitchen. I go directly for Mildred. She's making fries. I stand behind her for a minute or so, hiding, trying to breathe, before she says, turning, Who's my shadow?

Mil, I'm able to say, do I look all right?

She jiggles the deep-fry basket in the oil and then gives me a look-over. You look real good to me, she says.

My face, Mil, I say, take a look at my face. I look straight at her. I'm trying to get an honest view of the little piece of the world that is me—such a small piece, I think, to have such a volume of mess inside. It's your eyes, my mother said to me once in an inscrutable voice, I don't know what to make of your eyes. It was envy! Of my eyes. Of my *life*. And my being alive is not my fault—suddenly I know it—her envy is *not my fault!*

Your face looks real good, honey, says Mildred. You're a pretty girl, you know, and I know what I'm saying.

Mil, I need to know if something looks wrong with me.

Mil must be one of the geniuses. She takes time out. She sets aside the basket of fries and then faces me squarely, hands on hips. Jack, she calls, come over here a minute. Jack is in his undershirt. They stand side by side. Says Mil, Our Nan here wants to know if she looks all right.

Jack's response is a good-natured leer at me, but I don't care. I'm starting to breathe normally. Every minute that I'm safe inside this kitchen game is time to try and catch on to the mysteries.

You're not the fastest study, my theater teacher told me, but once you've got it, you're good, very, very good. That's what Mr. Calder saw; that's what he said when he was watching over me.

I don't want to cry right now in front of Mil and Jack. And I think I'm going to be able to do it—I mean the future. Just give me a minute.

Sweetheart, begins Jack, if I was a poet . . . I'd have to come up with some real beautiful words for you.

Mil jerks her thumb in his direction. Get him, isn't he something?

He sure is. I'm wiping off my cheeks; I'm crying anyway, but now I know the tears won't last too long because I'm already worried about whether my mascara is running.

I just need to sit a few minutes on this high work stool near Mil. I can hear Eddie singing over the sounds of the Hobart. This is the day-to-dayness of everything. It's not so bad. Watching Mil at work I notice more and more simply the motion of it, and the color, and then I'm imagining how if I had my camera with me I could go back out on the floor and expose a whole series on the ghoul. Click, click, me inside the skin of my own life, the camera picking up all the secrets I'm too slow to see now—they'd come out in the developing, maybe in the air around her head, what makes her strangeness, and my tears. I'd use the pictures to get brave enough for the circulation to go into her zone, and back home safe. Me, I'm not the perfect angel, but at least I don't have to be stuck. I can *learn*.

What I really have to do is get off this stool and go out and ask the ghoul if there is anything more she wants and give her a check. And there are all those other people waiting, my customers—my audience!

Thanks, Mil, I say, and I eat a couple of her fries to show her how much I love her, to show her I'm going to live.

Maybe the punks will get another treasure—who knows? Here I go, back into the thickness of people. Actually, I do love this, being in the middle of people. In college, away from home finally, when I started getting freed up by all those new individuals with their variety and energy, the really incredible energy of people learning, I was able to make my first macabre jokes about my mother. Is your mother big on discipline? someone might ask. Yes, I'd say, she's very stiff. Well, how do you get along? Oh, I'd answer, we've gotten along a lot better for the last five years.

All around me are voices.

Is that you, Brian? April! Hey, how're you anyway, what are you doing? Oh, I'm great—just living!

All around me are voices, and I'm moving straight into my work, but I don't know if I'm seeing what I'm seeing because the person sitting at the little table near the column is not an eerie, bad-smelling woman of uncertain age, but the Jerry person I sleep and talk and laugh and eat with—it really is Jerry, on his way to work probably, and here he is, making his forefingers into nubbins of seductive horns on either side of his head, which he does when he wants to tease me out of brooding into having some fun, but why did he sit down *there,* with her dirty Coney Dog plate in the opposite place? And that crafty ghoul got away without paying!

Jerry, how come you sat down at a dirty table? Glad as I am to see him, the first thing I say isn't very sweet, and I'm also thinking I ought to hustle him off to Eddie for decontamination. Come on, Jerry, there are other places to sit!

Yeah, well, today I'm mixing with the People, says Jerry. Your customer asked me to sit down with her.

She doesn't belong to me! I say. Jerry, that was the *ghoul.* And then I realize that I haven't told Jerry anything about her because we've barely had time to say hello-and-sleep-tight this week. Jerry, you don't know what you did, I say. This one is off the wall, she's a mutant, she's totally scary.

That's funny, says Jerry, because she's always spoken very highly of you.

Quit teasing! I say. This is really, really serious.

Jerry looks at me in a different way. Nan, hey, can you take a break? Sit down with me.

Not there! No, I can't, I just had my break.

I make myself pick up the ghoul's dirty dishes, intending to spirit them directly away at arm's length, but there on the table under the circle of the plate are some dollar bills.

See, says Jerry, she even left you a tip.

Not for me, I say, that's just for her gruesome Coney Dog.

When he reaches for the bills, I warn, Don't touch them, Jerry—they've got a half-life.

Now this is getting interesting, says Jerry in his let's-have-fun voice, and he starts to pick up the money.

My hands are full, and my squirrels are gibbering so much my wires are totally jammed. I walk away from Jerry and the money to the wait station, but just as I'm bending over by the bus pan, maybe getting a little extra blood to the brain, I say to myself that letting a ghoul get in the way of how I talk to Jerry is not something I have to be doing. Jerry is Jerry. And I'm me, I think as I stand up and wipe off my hands. I can make my next words different. I feel as if I've had one clear thought anyway.

I collect a few more dishes, take a few more orders, one from a woman with a set expression that reminds me an awful lot of Aunt Barbara, before I start back to take Jerry's. All around me are voices. Now my one clear thought is getting all mixed up with everything else. April and Brian are hitting it off. You should see me, April is saying as I pass their table, I've got my stuff in about five different places all over town!

What'll it be, I say in Betty's lingo when I get back to Jerry, but I know I'm not Betty, and I'm keeping my own eyes steady on his as the best thing I see, and I'm wishing that this entire overtired restaurant environment would dissolve into the beach where we'd be together in the wind, under the sun, running along the edge of the water beneath the many-colored aerobat, on the verge of a new world.

Look here, Nan, says Jerry. He has the dollar bills lined up on the table in front of him as if he's about to play a kids' board game. Then from under one of them he pulls out a black and white snapshot and holds it toward me. Your friend left you something.

Jerry, don't do this to me, I say. I'm trying not to look at the snapshot, but I'm glancing anyway, because the hand is after all Jerry's, and the form on the photo looks like a baby, one of us, a human being baby.

I clamp my eyes back on Jerry's and say, I want to know what this person said to you, exactly.

Not too much, says Jerry. First she motioned me over and said I could sit down because she was just leaving and this was an especially nice table.

Great, I say. So you sat down just like that? I'm starting to work my feet up and down in my hightops because all around me is the sound of the work I'm not doing.

Sure, so I sat down, says Jerry. I ask you, am I or am I not a student of people?

I want to know what she said, I demand.

First she just gave me the once-over, says Jerry. Then she said that I look like a nice enough young man.

I roll my eyes. What a line. It's almost funny. Then I take a second to glance over all the tables I'm not waiting on and catch sight of Annie and Ellen with their heads together by the planter, making big eyes at me and mouthing oo-oo because they know who Jerry is. I make a goofy face back at them, and then I'm thinking, what a clown you are, Nan, and suddenly, like a miracle, I'm almost all right. We're young, I think, Annie and Ellen, Jerry and I; we're ourselves inside our own time; we can turn it into whatever we want.

Annie and Ellen think you're cute, I say to Jerry, and he waves to them. He loves this.

And so it is that inside this moment that belongs to us, with my friends around me, I'm able to reach out and take the photo for a closer look—poor blotched, water-marked thing, it looks as if it has been through all the elements—poor baby crawling in diapers across the grass under the drooping branches of a weeping willow toward the camera—poor bare baby in a mottled picture, coming straight on toward the camera, unaware of me watching, her hands and knees working together alternately as they're supposed to, face up, forehead wrinkling: poor baby, she looks as if she's expecting the world.

There was a willow tree like that, I hear myself saying to Jerry. And there was a fence just like that one between the backyard and the alley.

Jerry rises halfway in his chair and cranes his neck for a better view.

Jerry, I think it's me. My hand is shaking, and my teeth are even chattering, as if I've been standing in the cooler for the last hour. I think the baby is me.

What are you talking about? says Jerry.

I keep looking at her. I think it's a picture of me as a baby, I say.

No, that's unreal, says Jerry. But he's standing close to me now. I feel his warm breathing, I feel the wonderful stature of him, close beside me.

I think it is, I say, still not able to take my eyes off her.

Baby, baby, creeping on all fours out of the old world, no hesitation, and she's not going to be able to change a thing. But wait a minute, wait a minute: I've lived through that already, haven't I? I don't have to go through it again! She may not be aware of me, but I see *her*. Baby, oh baby. I take one more long look, and then I put the picture in my apron pocket. This one, hot as it is, I'm not sending out again; it stops here, with me; I'm the one who's going to turn it into something else.

Not so fast! says Jerry. Let me see it again.

I slide out the photo and hand it back to him. My eyes are watching him as he looks closely at the little black and white shape, coming now straight toward him.

I don't get this, says Jerry. He's shaking his head over the picture, really concentrating.

Don't ask me, I say.

Finally a clearing smoothness passes into Jerry's face and he says, I think I'll take care of this little item if you don't mind, and he slips the picture into his shirt pocket, sits down again, takes up his menu, and smiles at me like a pleased customer. All right?

What are you going to do with it? I ask.

Trust me, he says.

I guess I'm pleased. Maybe this is how it feels to get a wish fulfilled, even one you didn't know you had. I'm holding my pen poised above my pad now, pretending to wait for his order. Jerry, I have to know, did she say anything else to you?

She just said that the food here is pretty good.

For a second my heart sort of bottoms out and even my squirrels seem outplayed, and then I say to myself, Okay, okay, keep going, just keep breathing, you're learning, even though one of the thousand thousand mysteries to you is how long she'll need to come around grubbing for satisfaction.

On my pad I write, *good food.*

THE EDGE OF TOWN

Overnight the last leaves of the twin maples in front of the house had fallen in one final shiver, and from the bedroom window a woman looked down through fog onto the damp black trunks rising out of two circles of reddish-gold. The gold struck heart, passing instantly through sight. Her name was Judith. This was how she was in the world these days, almost no breathing space between gold and heart. She was twenty-eight. One child was starting kindergarten, the other weaned but still in diapers. Could it simply be common motherhood, she wondered, that was rendering her so susceptible?

Barely morning, but Michael had already left for the laboratory. Last night he had come home at ten o'clock, straight from the electron microscope to their bed. How had her face looked, she had wondered, so close beneath him, real size? He was in a period of intense output, both in his research and in his new teaching job. It could be called overwork, or simply work, depending on the point of view.

She was staring so long that the two pools of reddish-gold were nearly converging. What she was made of, beside feeling, she couldn't think. If this state was commonplace, why was it

experienced as extreme? Somewhere she had read that the mind
was like the outer rim of the heart. Or was it the other way
around? Scientists, she told herself, constructed models on
which to base their investigations. All right, she could, too: she
would try to think reasonably about the mind being like the
outer rim of the heart, or the other way, the core of mind licking
out into a corona of emotion.

The sounds of the children waking almost seemed to come
from inside her own body. She was like a reflector for them of
themselves and at the same time a living accommodation. Each
day what she witnessed and made room for was much like that
of yesterday, yet sequential. If ever she had needed a lesson in
irreversibility she had gotten it with pregnancy; like an education inside the earth it was, all made up of mute sensation, only
one way out. But then the births themselves had become only
apparent disjunctions. Sequence led not out but deeper into par-
ticipation. The womb she lived in now, there was no end to it.
She was being made over, again and again.

What she could talk about with Michael and even with herself
was but the merest rim of what was happening to her as a result
of this intense contact with other bodies, this repetitious contact
with objects related to those other bodies, this cell-level aware-
ness at all times of the well-being of other bodies, inside the
womb of communion.

She hoped that she was still fairly sane.

The striped shirt or the blue one? she asked Peter. He would
wear the shirt he chose in his first worldly classroom. Nina, the
one to be left behind, knowing it, sat on his bed watching him
and kneading her fists into her favorite blanket, which was by
now, after only eighteen months, like a nearly colorless spider-
web. For the acceptance of her inventive and bossy brother she
would perform the services of a slave and trade nearly anything
but her blanket and her ratty pacifier. She loved him with no
earthly sense of justice or embarrassment. Without even ideas

about love, she just did it. Since he had begun departing each morning for the school bus, she had been like a moon, stunned by a disappearing sun. Maybe devotion had its place, Judith thought, or maybe it was just foolishness, its objects being so often imperfect.

The moment Peter disappeared out the side door after breakfast, Nina toddled in a rush to the living room and heaved herself into the old wing chair by the front window, where she stood pressed against its back to watch him reappear skipping down the front walk toward the maples. Why did she press herself like this against grief and loss, day after day? Judith followed and knelt into the chair, too; she talked quietly in Nina's ear, kissed her cheek, watched from behind, slightly to one side, the miraculously functioning, blue-irised eye of her baby daughter. From down the road came the yellow bus with its folding doors, its windows of bouncing faces, its trim purpose. Peter, confident now after over a month of such mornings, climbed on without looking back. Nina cried, almost ritualistically, and Judith did what she often did—put on music and picked Nina up and danced with her in the center of the nearly unfurnished room, circling and circling. The baby was still in her sleeping suit, and Judith was wearing clothes that might as well have been pajamas. These days she was still able to press a little yellowish milk from her nipples.

The collie growled and whined at the edge of the twirling with her nose between her paws, her wagging hind end in the air, until she sprang into her own frantic dance around them. The black cat leapt out of the way to the table. This melting room in which they turned must fit somehow into the surface of the world, but to Judith it felt as if she and the little body splayed against her chest were dancing toward an inner space that had its correspondence only in extraterrestrial vastness. At last, when the baby's stricken cries had turned to laughter, Judith collapsed with her into the second-hand chair, which was like a faded, frayed repository of human decades of emotions, its upholstered sides now fretted by the cat and its wooden claw and ball feet gnawed by the pup—but after all just a chair. The emotions had flown off somewhere else, like weather. What stayed?

Let's go find something just for you, said Judith.

The panting collie was watching them expectantly; the cat beneath the lamp appeared more self-contained.

Judith's own field of study had been history—that was to say, it was the field into which she had been planting a few tentative seeds, in the form of applications to graduate schools, at the time of her first pregnancy. The year had been 1965, and she and Michael had been unmarried when the laboratory report confirmed that a not-at-all tentative sperm, one half of the future Peter, had found a loophole in the clumsy science of birth control. So like Peter, they were to say to each other a few years later when his not-at-all-tentative character began to appear. And so much for science. Judith had not yet known anyone who had had an illegal abortion, though Michael had—one of his friends and a girl from his hometown. Michael had heard that the girl had gone mad, after the boy had been drafted and sent away and then killed. The baby might have saved them both, was Michael's comment. But Judith didn't want an abortion anyway. Here was love. Out there was war. Nothing was as important as being together. Not so long before, she had finally rolled over from the restraints of her girlhood, those from her long-unhappy, divorced mother nearly amounting to frantic taboos, into the brave new mode of trusting love, and at that time there was nothing to her of the same forthcoming reality as one body touching another. With Michael's chest as touchstone, her mind could sink into a quietness from which belled out a completion of worlds. The study of history, such as it had been defined so far, could wait, she had thought, while she let herself fall for a time into this deep roundness of self-discovery.

But of course history didn't wait for anything. In the course of events, Michael accepted his acceptance into graduate school; she declined hers, which would have been in another part of the country. They married in secret, two months before graduation, when they finally told their families. Judith's tight-lipped mother expressed the opinion that her daughter had already managed to accomplish a ruined life. Judith's father had long since disappeared from any contact with his child. Michael's parents came through with a small amount of money, but were explicit about their limits and the embarrassment caused them by the folly of this young generation, their own son in particular. Michael found scholarships and part-time jobs and other forms of financial assistance; Judith worked evenings and weekends in a library, when Michael could watch the baby, but was unable to find any other sort of child care they could afford.

But they were not grim. They were learning to adhere to each other, the three of them—then four. The second pregnancy they accepted as another lesson, another opportunity. What was the meaning of this new one that she could make everything seem even more real than before? And look how she was tempering Peter's fierce monopoly on childhood! Every day, of course, there was the business of the escalating war, the danger of the draft. They said to each other that if the generation of their parents, authors of the war, could not protect them from violation, then these babies might.

They lived in an apartment so small and with so few furnishings that when they moved a year ago for Michael's first teaching job, everything they owned fit easily into a friend's panel truck. Following behind in their own rattling car, they sang, they ate crackers and cheese and apples out of a basket, Judith nursed the baby like a pioneer en route—a pioneer woman.

And they were indeed going west, a little bit west. With her face tilted toward the extending countryside, her babies asleep, the journey underway, Judith had relaxed into a dreamy expansiveness. Being in thrall to life, in one way or another, was inescapable, she had thought. If not this, then it would be something else. When you were in life, that was what you had to work with—life. Her mind felt subtle as she savored the experience of thinking as an individual about universal existence. But no matter how far the mind expanded, she thought, there was no way inside life not to be on earth at a particular moment in time. She squinted toward the setting sun: context was everything, and then again nothing; history was alive, as it leapt back and forth between these poles. She wanted to study again.

So she spoke aloud to Michael: now that they were to have steadier money, as soon as they were settled in, she was going to find decent child care and then set herself toward going back to school. All right?

That was fine, it was what they had been talking about all along, said Michael. His voice was calm.

Whatever she did would mean changes for him, too, she said.

Of course, he said. Changes went with the territory.

She meant real changes. This was serious. She could hear her own voice rising.

Michael had reached over to stroke her arm, which was supporting the dead weight of the sleeping baby. He was with her, he said. All the way.

By the time the caravan of truck and car reached the old house Michael had rented on the eastern edge of the Midwestern university town, it was night, and her thoughts did not feel as subtle as they had in the flush of setting out—neither acute in particulars nor particularly inclusive. Perhaps nothing she had ever thought had had enough power to it. She felt the condition of knowing nothing. In the dark yard around the house, trees and overgrown bushes swayed in the fall wind. Leaves turned end over end in front of the headlights. Their friend jumped

from the truck and began signaling comically as if he were
berthing their airplane. This was a lark for him, maybe. He had
no family yet of his own. She wanted only to be put to bed. It
seemed incredible that before she could lie down, three beds had
to be carried across the yard and into an empty house and fitted
with sheets and blankets, two little children needed to be
soothed through the strangeness, two men would require her
energy and adaptation. She wanted only a singular blankness.

All thought eventually came down to the body, Judith was
thinking now as she bathed and dressed the baby. Each body
was in one life—except she herself doubted she was really one
body now. There was no way anymore she could calculate
where she stopped and the others began. Another image: the
cow jumping over the moon: could she have done it with dangling calves? Ask the scientists.

What she found for the baby this morning was the enticement
of the low cupboard of pots and pans. One by one, Nina began
carrying the utensils from the cupboard to a corner of the
kitchen floor. This might last twenty minutes. Judith started in
cleaning up the kitchen. Then she remembered the overdue rent
and stopped to write out a check and leave it in the door slot
before the mailman should come. Then she figured she had
enough time to go to the downstairs bathroom. She left the door
open so she could hear the baby just down the hall. Had she
remembered to close the cellar door? The kitchen was too quiet.

Nina, where are you, what are you doing? she called.

The collie came into the bathroom and tried to stick her wet
nose between Judith's legs. Go, said Judith, pushing her away,
go find the baby, what kind of nursemaid are you, anyway? Go
on, go on. The collie went only as far as the open doorway,
where she sat, studying Judith. Quickly Judith finished up. She
didn't take time to comb her hair. She found the baby inside the

cupboard, lying on her side, sucking her pacifier. Judith didn't know if this was an abject position or not. If someone else were in the room, she might feel embarrassed by the lonely hole into which her baby had crept. Hello, Nina baby, she called as she sat down at the kitchen table and took up the newspaper. Just ten minutes, she thought, ten minutes of empty sucking in the enclosure of a kitchen cupboard wasn't going to damage her baby for life.

A quick flurry of hope rose as she located the advertisement she herself had just placed in the classified section, for child care, two days a week, two children, references required, must have own transportation. She cut it out to show Michael. All year, while slowly making a home in a new community, she had also been trying to find acceptable child care. They had very little money available, but even that was not the most crucial circumstance. Of the handful of nursery schools in town, none would take a child still in diapers. For a brief, desperate time she had left both children for several mornings a week in the crowded home of an older, depressingly overweight woman, but withdrew them quickly when she noticed the glazed look in Peter's eyes and the baby's filthy diaper one day when she came to pick them up. It became unspeakable to her sometimes how alone she had been with this question. Even the other mothers in the park, to whom she had gradually introduced herself, could offer no solutions beyond the continually improvised mutual babysitting in which she joined now and then, but the segments of time offered were too brief, the arrangements too fraught with variables to allow her to commit herself beyond the family. In a larger town there might be more options, she thought, but this was where they were. The advertisement was another try: somewhere out there perhaps there was someone with a need into which her own could fit.

She pinned the scrap of newsprint above the telephone, and then just as she was starting to make herself read about the new deployment of troops, there was a knock at the back door, and she looked up to see the face of their next door neighbor in the glass, her heavy hair twisted up into a nonchalant bun. Elise was a caterer, specializing in wedding cakes. Her own fiancé had been killed in a motorcycle accident seven years before, and the boyfriend, Randy, who visited her now also drove a cycle. Elise wore the story of the tragic death like a permanent piece of almost glamorous clothing. It was one of the first things she had told Judith about herself, and from then on it was always visible. Lately Elise had been stopping by more often. Judith let her in.

Would you believe that I'm out of coffee? said Elise. Me of all people? She carried a pack of cigarettes.

Well, there's half a pot here, said Judith. Or would you like to take some beans home?

Oh, I'll have a cup with you, said Elise, stepping past Judith into the room. Her black ribbed sweater, her dangling earrings, her jeans, her Western boots—there was art beneath this insouciance, Judith knew. In her own sweatshirt and jeans she suddenly felt like a cave woman. Elise was sweeping her eyes about the kitchen as Judith fetched mugs and poured the coffee.

Oh! What's your baby doing in the cupboard?

Sucking her pacifier, said Judith.

How cute, said Elise. She sighed and sat down at the table. I shouldn't drink so much wine at night, I really shouldn't because I swell up something terrible. Cigarette?

No, thanks, said Judith as she nudged the cat from the table and cleared off the newspapers.

Oh come on, join the old lady in a smoke. Live dangerously.

I've already lived dangerously, said Judith. I don't want to anymore.

You? Elise laughed. Judith, you're a girl scout if I've ever seen one. Well, it's going to be dangerous whether you want it to be or not. Everything's dangerous. She took a deep drag on her cigarette and blew the smoke toward the ceiling. Has Michael left yet? She balanced her cigarette on the edge of the baby's drying cereal bowl so she could reposition the combs in her hair—beautiful auburn hair. Judith had once told her so, and Elise had answered that, yes, there were several things about herself that she liked quite a lot.

Hours ago, said Judith. Dawn. He's got some things cooking in the lab.

The baby crawled out of the cupboard and made straight for Judith's lap. Judith teased the pacifier out of her mouth.

Your baby is looking more and more like Michael, said Elise. I really can't see you in her at all.

Really? My mother might take issue with that.

Oh, well, mothers, said Elise. Can you ever believe them?

I don't know, said Judith. She didn't want to think just then about all the sadness that had come to her from her mother and about all the effort that was being required to disbelieve it.

Let me hold her, said Elise, reaching for Nina. She leaned closer, her complicated earrings swaying, and the baby was entranced. Such a sweetie, such a little Michael. Elise began bouncing the baby. A dull confusion was settling upon Judith. Her lap felt empty.

Did Michael tell you I gave him a ride the other day when he ran out of gas? There he was trudging along River Street with the gas can and luckily I was on my way to deliver a cake.

No, he didn't tell me, said Judith. A lot happens that we don't get a chance to talk about.

Mm, I suppose so, said Elise. And then it was so funny that a few minutes later we caught sight of you.

Of me? said Judith. What do you mean?

Elise was still bouncing the baby, holding the tiny grabbing hands in both of hers to save her earrings. You were at the swings in the park with the kids. I said, Duck quick, Michael, there's your wife over there!

Why would you ever want to say that? said Judith. She had gotten up to fill the baby's bottle, and in an instant, as soon as Nina saw the milk, Judith had her arms full once more.

Oh, just to be silly, said Elise. She picked up her cigarette again. I was in such a crazy mood that day.

Well, I wish you had stopped, said Judith. I was getting cold that afternoon. The wind was coming up.

Oh, I was in a ferocious hurry to deliver the cake, said Elise. Honestly, Judith, you wouldn't believe the kind of hours I keep sometimes and the kind of demands people put on me. Now that particular cake took all night and half the wedding day. Do you know what Michael said when he saw it? He said if I could make a structure like that with eggs and flour, he'd like to see what I could do with steel and concrete. He said I should go to architecture school. Sweet man, but what does he know, right? Now how is someone like me, no money and zero in the math department, going to get herself to architecture school?

Have you ever thought about it? asked Judith. Her thoughts were so scrambled and emotional she could barely speak.

Elise began to talk again, but now there was such a roaring inside Judith that all she could hear were the interior words she had begun to ask herself: after he had gotten the gas, why hadn't he come back to the park for her and the children, since he knew they were there? Why had she had to walk home alone in the five o'clock wind, pushing the stroller, Peter wheeling behind? Where had he gone then? Where did he think he was going, every day and every day? And that was just the beginning of the questions. She tried to concentrate on the sound of the baby sucking. She felt nauseated by the cigarette smoke. She thought she heard Elise say something about a sugar daddy in the sky. That surely couldn't be Randy.

Tell me, Judith, I bet Michael was your first love, wasn't he?

Judith looked flatly across at her neighbor, the woman she had thought was becoming her friend. She was asking her own mind to work, or her heart, whatever was needed, but she didn't seem to have the structures available to deal with what was happening. What was happening? She said nothing.

Elise sighed. Never mind, she said. I was like you once. Everything can change overnight, that's what I know now. You can't ever go back. Of course, who would want to? You'd just have to go through all that garbage again, right?

Then, astonishingly, Elise folded her arms on the table and laid her head on them. Oh me, I do have to stop drinking wine. I don't like myself this way. Your kitchen is nice, Judith. I think I could go to sleep right here.

Oh, you'd be far more comfortable in your own bed, I'm sure, said Judith with an exaggerated, undermined politeness her mother might have admired. Please excuse me, I'm going upstairs to change the baby. She stood with her child in her arms, tall now above the figure of Elise. Behind her eyes, the confusion was gathering into an utterly new force that felt like a weapon. In the absence of Michael, the ultimate object of her questions, this force took the form of a devastating calm that she inflicted upon the gorgeous loose coil of hair and slumping shoulders of Elise. Please do help yourself to more coffee before you leave, Elise, she said. And then she walked from the room, singing to the baby.

She sang all the way up the stairs, Here we go loop de loo; she sang while she changed the diaper; she sang while she folded a few clothes, nursery rhymes, nonsense songs, love songs, anything that came to mind; she sang until she thought she heard the back door close, and then suddenly she was silent.

By the time the school bus appeared at noon, the fog had turned to a steady rain, streaming down the windows, drumming on all the fallen leaves. With an energy conjured out of will, Judith

ran down the front walk under the umbrella and was waiting as
the bus doors unfolded and Peter jumped down.

There's Nina waving at you, she instructed, and they both
waved through the rain at the little head in the window.

Let Elise watch, Judith was thinking. Let her look across the
yard and watch me caring for the children I have made with
Michael. Let her know the human gold in defense of which my
strength could make her drown in her own covetous blood. And
all the time her own heart was beating, no, no, no, no, not such
a stupidity as that, not from him, not now, not ever.

She cooked carrots and rice. She spooned applesauce into the
baby. She made herself listen and answer. She heard three
voices. From somewhere in outer space she heard the voices of
two children and a mother in the kitchen of an old house deep
inside a bleary October afternoon on earth. She washed off the
highchair tray. She washed the dishes. She swept the kitchen
floor. She set out bowls of fresh water for the dog and cat. Then
she turned out the lights in the kitchen and in the dining room,
where both children were playing under the table.

No! cried Peter.

Yes, she said. We're all going upstairs now to rest. Bring
some of your soldiers with you if you want to play on your
bed.

I can't move the game! protested Peter more loudly.

Then leave it, she said firmly. This is it. If I don't have a nap
right now, I'm going to die. And then she thought, Oh god,
he'll probably be marked forever by his mother's drastic language. She crawled under the table for the baby, who was practically asleep anyway. Peter had assigned Nina a place on the
perimeter of his game and given her a few small toys to hold.
With these she sat, bunching up the satin of her blanket and
sucking her pacifier. Come along, Peter, said Judith, backing out
in a crouch with the baby in her arms. As soon as we've all had
a good rest, I'll read to you.

Mi-mi, said the baby, holding the wadded blanket up for Judith to smell.

Delicious, said Judith as she nuzzled into the softness of her child. Sweetest thing on earth. Sweetest and sweetest and sweetest. She was dazed by tiredness. She kept the words coming to keep her legs moving up the stairs, to keep her hands moving as she changed another diaper and lowered the baby into the crib. Sweet sleep, she said. She spread another blanket over the baby. See how sweet your sleep is? she whispered because the baby's eyes were already closing.

Where was Michael in this sequence of daily events? And where, where was the father she had never seen again?

Peter, she called down the stairs. One, two, three, I mean it. Miraculously, he came. But he refused to be in his own bed. I want to be in yours, he said.

How quiet can you be? she asked.

Quiet, said Peter. He marched off and brought back a stack of books, two stuffed animals, Overmouse and Underdog, and a shoe box of plastic monsters and prehistoric animals. He climbed up and arranged himself on Michael's side of the bed.

I'm trusting you, Peter, she said. No explosions, no creatures crawling over my face, nothing—understand?

His grin was so characteristic—self-absorbed, determined, vividly intelligent—that she felt a moment of almost disinvolved appreciation of him before she remembered that in the course of the small history of Peter, a woman not herself would most likely be one day in this very place next to him. For the sake of this woman of the future, now a girl child somewhere else, what were the questions Judith herself could be putting before her son? He was a real person already, she thought—everything needed was already there, in the process of developing, yet each step of the way he needed to be questioned. Everything needed to be questioned.

But what she did for the moment, out of her appreciation, out of her exhaustion, was simply to say, You're a great kid, Peter, before she kissed him on the cheek and rolled over and hid herself under the quilt.

Oh, didn't Michael miss being with them? Judith closed her eyes. Her first outward breaths were almost like soft moans. *Here* was love. Michael had made promises to be involved. They had made promises to each other, one individual to another, to stay involved in the larger enterprise of what they said they were making, a family. He was the one, first of all, the mate from her generation, with whom she needed to talk. She heard herself beginning: Michael, believe me, listen to me: infidelities of every kind accumulate into war. She moaned again. She felt she could bore a hole in the bed with her fatigue and with the force of the questions she was being impelled by circumstances to ask.

Her direction was downward, as if into the earth again, to retrieve another, forgotten part of her education. Maybe she would never be done with this process of being born. And it was all she had to work with, the life of this one person who had to keep going back in to be remade.

Peter wasn't especially quiet, but it didn't seem to matter. Nor did it matter that the dog pushed her way through the crack in the door, lifted her nose over the edge of the bed and whined into the blanketed shape of Judith's body before finally settling down on the rug beside the bed. Judith felt the cat thud softly onto the quilt and curl into the angle of her folded legs. Peter was reading to himself, a sort of singsong that was a mixture of the words he really could read, those he remembered having been read to him, and those he added for his private embellishment. His breathy chanting even seemed to keep the surface steadier so that she could continue in her downward penetration to the bedrock question of love, which had turned molten again, overnight. Before the question was where she would be waiting and listening. She wanted to go beyond all emotions, all forms of thought. Just to be alive, asking the question, might be enough. For an instant, she felt absolute, impervious; she thought she might have the courage to wait forever, listening to the silence.

But then the next moment she was remembering a story Elise told her one hot summer afternoon, just a few months ago, when they had been sitting side by side in lawn chairs watching the children play in the wading pool—Elise whose company she had been glad for, Elise whom she did not want to dislike. It was a story, Elise had said, to take their minds off the heat of the day.

It took place when her fiancé had been dead a week. They had both been twenty-four. Ordinary days were supposed to resume, but Elise in her desperate state thought that for her this would never be possible again. It was January, one of the coldest nights of the year. Elise waited until everyone was asleep in the house of her parents. Then she dressed herself in winter coat, boots, hat, scarf, gloves, everything she would have worn had she been intending to keep herself alive. She slipped out of the house and walked the blocks to the frigid great lake. It was a clear night, she said, icy stars above, ice below. Her intention was to lie down on the beach under the sky beside the sloshing fields of ice and wait to freeze to death. It was a passionate intention. All her emotions had come together into something she could do. She arrived at the beach. She lay down near the rim of the ice, drawing her legs up under her coat. She began to wait.

Well? Then? Judith had demanded. What happened next?

Elise had laughed. Her face, her bare arms, her legs glistened with perspiration. The children were shrieking in the water. Oh, you know me, she said. I just got cold and wanted to go home.

AFTERNOONS, CORRIDORS

I live in the neighborhood of plain work. For a long time that has been pretty much what I settle into, like this classroom, for instance, the blackboards on three walls, the heavy old windows, a stack of one-page essays in front of me. I am content, though of late I do seem to be woolgathering rather more than usual, which is surprising to me. I remember even my childhood as a kind of work.

This time of year I let the bottom panels of the classroom windows fall open on their chains. There's often a wind in the trees; it's hard for me not to stare into the newly leaved branches and do nothing. One of my longtime friends, from childhood, is turning out to be something of a mystic. It's strange to be learning this now because Lois has always been one of the most pragmatic and competent people I've known. She and her husband are often on my mind these days because of Hugh's illness, and because of what Lois has been telling me.

In the afternoons when the seventh-graders leave, I usually stay at my desk in the vacant classroom for several hours. I find it is more efficient to read their compositions and grammar exercises right here on the field reverberating with our voices,

when I'm still more or less on my mettle. A language arts
teacher has to maintain an awfully high level of belief in words,
like a dervish in the classroom, I see her, trying to keep in
motion the whole dancing enterprise of speech. I do it, time
and again, at least someone is up there doing it, but I still hav-
en't decided, at the age of fifty-five, whether or not it's me. It
must be.

My pleasure in the silence of the school building as I leave
each day—the empty hallways, the door after door of empty
classrooms, the nearly deserted parking lot—can feel almost
subversive. Why persist in using language, I sometimes whisper
inside myself, when silence is so sweet? It's a good thing I try
not to take much work home. Lately, more and more, pedagog-
ical fervor seems to leak away from me during the encapsulated
twenty minutes in my car to the little driveway, the yews, the
neat, brick house where I live with Norman. From here I see
our checkered-wallpaper kitchen where nothing but the light
will have changed since morning. If Norm isn't home yet, I
often just sit for a while before starting dinner. I don't do anything. Even when he comes in the door, life is made fairly simple by our regular routines. Now that our daughter Joyce is
grown, we live almost like affectionate monastics, he and I.
Norm says our marriage has achieved many of the advantages
of living alone.

I lost my father when I was still in high school, and my
mother died about ten years ago; they were both middle-aged
when I was born, their only child. I'm older now than my father
ever was. I don't know if he'd recognize me. Life surprised him,
too, I imagine, and so must his abrupt death have. He was almost as quiet before as after, but as a girl I missed him horribly.
Who else was there now for my mother to criticize besides me?
I was fortunate, I suppose, that there were so many Good
Works absorbing her energies; she was lucky that she could
afford to indulge in them. But I don't believe she ever consid-

ered herself fortunate. For one thing, I was never the child she seemed to have been expecting, and the older I got, the less inclined I was to attempt to appease her disappointment. Except for teaching and raising a child and being a companion to Norman, all which I have generally liked very much, I have not done many good works myself. Lois has.

The wind beyond the windows has business with the trees this afternoon, fluctuating movement, this way, that way. Most of my life I've kept fairly busy. I've tried to find a few ways to please myself and at the same time be useful and unobjectionable. I like ordinary tasks; I've grown not to care so much whether or not anyone else actually notices when I'm being productive or even generous. I just know when I feel good enough for me, and I stick to doing those things. During this coming summer vacation I plan to paint the fence and build a rock garden on the slope at the end of the perennial bed. We'll take care of Joyce and Harry's little boys for two weeks so that Joyce can get to her convention and afterward have a vacation with Harry. They get tired, I know, those young parents.

I may also get to sorting through those boxes of Mother's things in the attic, which I've been putting off these ten years. It will be hot up there, though. Maybe I should carry everything downstairs and make enough of a mess so that I have no choice but to carry through.

The garden can be so beautiful. Even small as it is, it's enough for me. In the warm weather I like to drink my breakfast coffee out there in the backyard and read for an hour or so. Or maybe I'm not reading every minute; maybe I'm just sitting. I am probably a bit too fond of coffee, but I say it's impossible to be too fond of a garden. Right now the tulips are ending, the iris and peonies beginning, the delphiniums and veronica and feverfew pushing up to be next. Then lilies, yarrow, bee balm, on and on. We often have our dinner in the garden, too. I like to stay outside until the trees are almost black against what is left of blue in the sky. When we go inside, Norman, my own electrical engineer, makes a ritual of going about the downstairs turning on lamps, according to his ingenious system of switches.

Norman and I do talk, of course, we take walks before bed, we have our lovemaking, we talk from our pillows in the dark, we talk as we get through the housework without much fuss, our somewhat segregated tasks. I have loved Norman over and over again for his steady good humor, and most of all for his acceptance of me. I simply like to sit in the same room with him. When he is concentrating, his whole vicinity can seem orderly—I wish some of my students could learn from the pleasure he takes, a pleasure serious and calm and matter-of-fact, when he is absorbed.

We both like movies, but I do read more than Norman does, and I can only turn on the opera when he's not home. The singers, he says, take too long to say it. In general, he prefers quiet to music or talk. Even when he's in his repair shop in the basement, he rarely listens to the radio; I like to think that solving material problems might set up a sort of pleasing rhythm of its own in his head. At any rate, he's usually happy when he comes back upstairs. It is not unusual for him to draw schematic diagrams of circuits on the backs of envelopes while he's sitting at the kitchen table waiting for his dinner, though he will raise his head from these lines and connection nodes and arrows and squiggles—like strange little floor plans they seem—and talk to me if I get going on something I need to say.

When I'm alone in the house I occasionally sing to myself. Once, when Joyce overheard me, she said I sounded like a nun in a stone room. Actually, I had been happy, singing in that minor way. I supposed I should be gratified that at least she hadn't asked me to lighten up. Then I looked over at her—she was smiling; she liked me all right, I guessed, even as I was—and I was happy enough again. After my childhood, I know I am fortunate to be connected to this husband and this child. I am also fortunate in my friends. We're here together for a short time—we feel this now—and the people I love best seem glad simply to be alive at the same time.

For most of our adult lives my friend Lois and I have had to carry on our conversations by telephone, long-distance. These last six months we have been talking much more than usual, no doubt because of Hugh, but it also might be our particular age, and we've always been the same age as each other, both of us going through the same critical stages together. It's a kind of education, our friendship. We've known each other since fourth grade, her mother was our girl scout troop leader, we went to summer camp together for a number of years, I adored their lively family and their kennel of Irish setters out back, so different from my own home. After high school we continued calling each other late at night from our respective colleges, and when our children were growing up we'd organize reunions of our two families now and then—these voices of ours go way back.

Pragmatism, I think, has been more than a necessity with Lois. The necessity part is that she and Hugh are both lawyers, they have raised four children; for the last thirty years Lois's brother Bill has been manic-depressive, careening in and out of her life, needing her attention, and now still alongside her is a radically changed husband, one side of his forehead slightly concave since the removal of the tumor, not many mental functions left completely unimpaired. His brain doesn't feel the same, he has told her, but he knows he still has his mind. I try to imagine being Hugh. How remarkable—to be so conscious of loss and yet feel whole. He's lucky he had so much to start out with, Lois says matter-of-factly. She really is a genius at accepting whatever is happening, rearranging what she can, if she needs to, and then just making the rest work, somehow.

Pragmatism, yes, but now that I am hearing about her mystical experiences, I am coming to realize that she may have organized herself so well all these years not just because she has had to with such a full plate of responsibility, but because she has also sensed all along what may be out there in the air, so to speak, like surprising winds, unexpected laws, waiting to be grounded through human beings. She's like a tree, I think, which for every outward-reaching branch grows a stabilizing root.

I think she's turning into one of the wise ones. When I told her this on the telephone one night, shortly after I had flown out to be with her during Hugh's operation and we knew that he would live—the tumor though large was fairly well encapsulated and benign—but that it would never again be life as before, she answered that all she really feels she's learning is to be a little more familiar with the unknown, to recognize it. It is not at all what she expected, and yet it is still a livable life. Besides, she told me, what are experiences? Knowledge doesn't spring directly out of experiences. You can have all the experiences in the world, she said, and still not know what is essential. It must be grace, she thinks, that enters in. Then she was uncharacteristically quiet. I was avid for her to say more. How do you get more familiar with the unknown? I finally demanded, like a child. All I can tell you is that it's coming toward me, she said, there's nothing I can do to stop it, and I guess I'm just sort of learning to lean into it.

It would be interesting to compute the telephone hours Lois and I have logged together over the years—equal to a term of college? More? Those two mystics, Bell and Watson, might enjoy knowing what latter-day uses we have made of their electronic invention. In the past there were periods when we were too busy to talk or strangely didn't have much to say, but then something would happen to jolt us into needing to put a question to the other, simply hear the sound of the other, or the sound of the past, maybe an inkling of the future.

The future is always going to be different than one can even imagine; if I didn't know this before, I've learned it for certain through Lois and Hugh. And Bill. Who of us back then could have imagined that Bill with his intelligence would become a victim of himself? For a while in high school I fantasized about marrying Bill. I wanted to be a permanent part of that family; I didn't want anything to change. Then came the bridge, the jump, the river, the chance rescue from the ice floes, the hospital, over and over, electroshock, a parade of drugs. He cannot keep a job. When I last saw him he was pasty, fat, perspiring.

My classroom may look the same to me, my kitchen and garden may look the same, almost, but nowadays, knowing how altered life can become and still be life, I step along in a slightly different way. What I didn't expect at all was this much air everywhere; it's even underfoot.

One of the anomalies of Hugh's impaired brain functioning, which became apparent soon after the operation, was that he was able to write down his thoughts, in a somewhat scrambled form, but was unable to read. But I'm still in the language, he has told her. To be alive and not be "in a language"—this I have been trying to imagine, and it's like being a child and trying to think for the first time of stars beyond stars beyond stars, on and on, which is something Lois and I used to do at summer camp, lying flat on our backs under the open night sky. For several months Hugh has been attending a special school, at his age, to try to relearn the alphabet, the ideas of syllables, phonetics, the whole thing. He gets awfully worn out and frustrated, Lois says, but except for a terrible night of rage after the angiogram, before the surgery, he has not seemed angry at his whole situation, except now and then his voice gets very loud. He doesn't shout or hit or throw things; he just talks very loudly for a few minutes, and then he calms down. He's extraordinarily affectionate. I think he loves me more now, Lois was saying the other night, almost in a whisper, I think he actually loves me more now. And he wants to make love nearly every night.

Bed is too small for my tiredness, we used to sing under the stars at the top of our indefatigable ten-year-old camper voices, *Give me a hill topped with trees, Tuck a cloud up under my chin; Lord, blow the moon out, please.*

I doubt that many other people know Lois as I do. The public side of her has always made such a neat, energetic package. For many years she has been vigorously engaged in community affairs—schools, social justice, legislation affecting the mentally ill—but now she has cut back on some of her activities so that their daily routine can be regular for Hugh. It's the way you like to live, Martha, she told me, you'd approve—bed early, meals at the same times, everything put back in the same logical place. She wasn't really making fun of me; all our lives we've kidded each other about our differences. I'm the centripetal one, like a dog turning around and around and at last lying down to sleep each night in the same spot. Lois isn't really the opposite —she's not flying off anywhere—but she has always overextended herself, lived on the fringes of her energy, loved the feeling of using up everything she has in the service of something she considered larger than herself. It's a brand of good works that's a good bit more bracing to hear about than my mother's used to be.

It's strange to have had such a vociferous mother as mine and still, even at my age, want another one.

So Lois has cut back on many of her community activities, but she's keeping her hand in one service project. A few years ago she became one of the creators and legal advisors of a trust fund program that aging parents of modest means can use to supplement but not jeopardize state aid to physically or mentally disabled children. A nasty underside of the trend toward community mainstreaming of the disabled, she says, is that when their parents die, the middle-aged children often end up as street people. Her advocacy for this cause grew out of her experiences with Bill, of course, but ironically the benefits of such a program would now extend to Hugh, should Lois die before him. For so many years most people have seen her in the midst of actions such as these. How many others, I wonder, have been allowed the glimpses of her that have fed my own life?

I was the one to whom a year ago she sent those eerily beautiful drawings she found in the waste basket by Hugh's desk, in retrospect the first signs of his tumor, drawings that seemed to have issued from the hand of an aerial cartographer suddenly launched into an orbit all his own. I'm perhaps the only witness who has been able to see these six months of her devotion to Hugh against a history of reddish dogs let out of the kennels and racing for joy on a hill of grass, of rows and rows of campers with crowns of glorious hot hair standing on the bleachers in the sun for the group picture, of the sound of a late-night train wailing and rushing through the telephone connection of two college girls—Whose end is that train on? she asked, and for a moment neither of us knew. These were moments that catapulted me into euphoria. I still have their flavor.

But I've never had a real vision. Lois has. Thirty years ago it came to her, and I have only learned of it now. Maybe I'm one of the few to know. A luminous figure. Someone else, she said to me in the hospital waiting room, might well supply a different name; Christ was what came to her. It had taken her until the day of Hugh's surgery to give me the story.

Why until now? I asked. I couldn't quite put together what she was saying with everything else that was happening. All around us was the steady bustle of a metropolitan teaching hospital. Under that very roof were probably examples of the most lost of souls, the most self-important of personalities, cruelty, kindness, indifference, attention. Even miracles, perhaps. Visions.

I got busy, it got lost, she said. She even shrugged. It just got misted over. Now I'm telling you.

All these years I could have been thinking about it, I said. I was amazed that we were able to talk at a time like this; I was amazed that we were talking this way. What else are you holding back? I asked her. It almost felt as if we were ten years old again.

We were sitting close on those awful plastic chairs in the sixth floor waiting room, gripping each other's hands. I had just gotten in from the airport. Maybe we were using our voices to make ourselves real. No one else spoke to us, as if there were a code not to approach the family of the person in surgery. The jury was still out. Two of her sons arrived in a little while, and then there were four of us waiting, in our terrible privacy.

But before her sons arrived, she told me the story. The figure she called Christ, apparently made of light, came to her in law school, in the library. It had been June, she thought. Anyway, there was still some sunlight slanting along the corridors of stacked books when she returned from dinner to her studying. As she told me, she used the word *slanting* and then even laughed, in that harshly lit hospital setting, about how poets often use *slanting* to talk about time, or eternity, or the zone between, and then she quoted Emily Dickinson and Rilke, something about this slanting hour in which you see me hurry so. She gripped my hands; her voice was almost rushed, as if at this moment she was compelled to establish herself firmly on this side, the side of sound, of time and swift speech.

At first, she said, seeing the figure, she thought she might have been drinking too much coffee, staying up too late, repressing her sexual feelings, whatever, and now her mind was playing tricks on her. She stood transfixed in the library stacks, one section of books away, until the figure dissolved. He had been looking directly at her, she remembers—at least she felt absolutely connected. Afterwards, the library looked complete and beautiful. She says her feet must have walked her to her carrel, which was also in the evening sunlight. There was, in fact, so much sunlight on the desk that she could barely make out the words on the page. She remembers feeling intensely happy. It was this intense happiness that told her something had actually happened. At the time she accepted this as a fact, she said. She closed her eyes and accepted it. Something had happened. Then, very characteristically, she rearranged her books and started studying again.

And then you really forgot about it? I wanted to know. How can you forget something like that?

Oh, I glimpsed it now and then over the years, she said, but it did sort of dissolve in my mind. I didn't dwell on it. Who would have believed it?

I surprised myself by saying, You could have told Bill. I was seeing him as he used to be, lean and bright and urgent, made into a star by that affable family, and for a moment I wanted everything back, exactly as it had been, even myself. I was forgetting that by the time Lois was in law school, I was married to Norman, and Bill had already been sucked into the convolutions of his illness.

Oh, Bill! she said. Maybe I was scared I was turning into another Bill. That's all my parents would have needed—two of us going off the deep end.

You could have told me, I ventured to say. You could have called me long distance.

She looked at me completely. It was a slow moment. I was having a hard time believing that we were really in our fifties, she and I, and that we had no idea how much longer we would be alive to be friends.

Yes, I could have told you, she said, but I don't think I was remembering it enough to talk about it, until now, really, Martha—and here she gripped my hands even tighter. I don't know how I can be talking so much today when everything is supposedly so unspeakable. I didn't sleep last night. I floated. This morning I thought I would be exhausted, but I don't feel exhausted. I don't understand what's happening. It's almost as if I'm floating now. On the way to the hospital in the car, by myself, when I was thinking of Hugh, head shaved, drugged, waiting, the sad real picture, the memory of the old vision came to me again complete, and it was almost as if it were happening again. It did happen back then, I'm pretty sure of that. I can't say it didn't.

Then she stopped talking and looked around her, and I had to look, too, at the place humans in this part of the world call a healing place. Lois released her hands from mine and placed her fingertips on her forehead. Why should I remember the whole thing *today?* she said. Everything is right here. She held her forehead in a cage of fingers. It's all happening at once, she said. And then she was crying, the first time I had heard her cry since she and Hugh had been told that an operation was the only hope. Martha, she cried, why *his* brain?

Something was telling me not to touch her until her face had passed through these contortions of grief. I knew this face—the usually calm brow, the olive skin, the square jaw—I had seen this face pass through nearly half a century. After a while I put my arms around her. Now you have remembered, was all I could say to her.

Then in a little while her sons came and we waited and waited. The surgery took ten hours, four longer than expected. Everything dissolved into waiting and not knowing.

Since then, back in my own life, I've been turning the story over and over in my mind. I've asked her to repeat it for me several times on the telephone; I don't know if this is for me, who like a child wants to hear a favorite story over and over, or whether I want to make sure that she herself will never forget it again. The other night I asked her if she had told Hugh.

I did, she said. And he did seem to get the picture.

What did he say? I asked.

He said that the figure was a guest, and I said to him, You mean ghost? And he said, One of those. It's like he's talking poetry most of the time, Martha. When he can't locate a word he wants—maybe literally it was cut away, that's what it seems like to me—then he substitutes another, and usually the meaning he ends up with is more expansive than it would have been if he had used the word he'd wanted in the first place. He's so proud of Stephen for getting his article published, and the word he uses is publicked. When he was thirsty, he asked for a vast of water. What is this area called? he asked me—he knows there's a wildness to his words. This area? I said. You mean this room? He said, No, I mean this area where we're not dead. You mean life? I said. Yes, he said, that's it. The other night he was standing at the foot of our bed holding onto one of the high posts. What is this? he asked me. Bedpost? I said. Bed? I was going to say trolley, he said, I was going to ask you to get in the trolley.

I picture them together, their bodies together, Hugh's body wanting her with uncompromised simplicity and immediacy. When I look at Norman's forehead close to mine, I think of his brain with its circuitry intact; I wonder if he's solving problems of his own, as I sometimes am, while we're making love.

These afternoons pass one into another. Sometimes it is raining hard and I have to close the windows, but if the rain is gentle I just leave them open and watch the countless downward dashes of water. One afternoon I cried because Dexter Thornton had written an essay so much better than I had expected out of him, about Pop, his grandfather, and his way of pursing his lips and blowing out and then saying, So it goes, so it goes. This boy is awake in his heart, I thought, and he even got his objective case pronouns right. I started thinking about the look of Dexter Thornton folded into one of the desks, his long legs in jeans, his smooth dark brown arms resting on either side of his book, his still-thin shoulders hunched in a T-shirt, his very nice face with dark eyes sometimes paying good attention. I was thinking how I love this student, how I have loved many students, how I have felt their love sometimes, have let them love me, have used this love to charm them into wanting to do their work. Some people have told me I must be crazy to want to teach seventh-graders, and I say, well maybe, but look, this is the moment when you can really see who they were and who they might become—the baby is still there, so clearly, and also the woman, the man, everything is present, everything is possible. Not with today's kids, some people say, most of them are wasted before they're out of the grades. I don't believe that, I tell them. Anyway, what other work could I do and still have the fun of diagramming sentences year after year?

Hugh says you don't know anything about time until you've been under the continual lights of Intensive Care.

Last night I was paying bills at the desk in the dining room and Norman was doing dishes. Come here, Marth, he called to me from the sink. My mind was on the little columns of figures in my checkbook. I asked him why. Just come here please, he said. I got up and went into the kitchen. It's this scrambled egg pan, he said, it smells like a wet dog. I bent over the sink. He was right. He was astonishing. Or maybe it was myself I found astonishing. I was astonished how much I loved us both. And I was missing our dead spaniel. Norman must have been, too, because he doesn't often say things like that.

It was such a surprise to me, after I had been teaching for a while, when I realized that some students would love me. I hadn't expected this, though I should have because I still feel love for some of my teachers from long ago, for the ways in which they saved my life. I would imagine my mother suddenly appearing at the back of my classroom and seeing how this love was working, how the daughter she had called ungrateful and disrespectful, indolent and sassy, was at work in the world. I wanted her to hear the voices, quick on the uptake, calling out the parts of speech; I wanted her to see me cooperating with a team of teachers, on something like that Inland Waterways unit we just did, for example; I wanted her to watch me in my marriage, enjoying myself fairly well and not wasting too much time on judgments. I read you like a book, she used to tell me, but she didn't; it seemed to me she barely saw what my story could be. Could she, I used to wonder as an adult, read me now?

But my mother didn't appear in the back of the classroom; I found I was on my own, just doing my work. I stopped imagining scenes in which I was proving to her that I had seized my own life. Her opinions meant less and less to me. Toward the end nothing was concealing her bitterness. Even Good Works were no longer palliations. Her mouth clamped into its final expressions. But then one day she said to me, with wonderful articulateness, Time has darkened everything except my hair, and I had to recollect that out of her, as well as my father, had come my language, my physical body and my body of language. And it braced me up that she was not losing her mind. Silently, I used to cheer her on, Don't lose your marbles, at least don't lose your marbles. And she never did.

It wouldn't be at all fair of me to leave those boxes of Mother's things for Joyce. I could do that, shove them way to the back of the luggage closet and never look at them again. One hot day when she was about my age now, Joyce would climb to the attic with some empty boxes and garbage bags. Danny and Mickey would be grown. I would have walked out the back door into the garden and died. Another generation would have passed. It would be for Joyce to choose what she could use and to throw the rest away.

Late afternoons hold a quality I want more of—what it is? Breathlessness? From half a building away I can hear the orchestra practicing for graduation, too far away for me to feel anxious over their intonation. New textbooks for next year have already arrived, new grammar workbooks. For years I have read grammar books for fun. What am I still doing, filling my head this way with hundreds of ways of circling around the same thing? The Simplest Complete Thought: that's one chapter heading. Ha, tell me about it. I'd really like to know what it is.

Being in a language and using words is like using life to find out about being alive. It's all you've got; you turn around and around in the middle of it and do the best you can. But, as Lois says, something more is needed than an accumulation of experience. Grace—is that it? Meanwhile, I'm looking at the new books. I'm trying to work up a decent anticipation for next year.

Something happened to me last night, but first I talked with Lois, who called about eight-thirty; Norman finished up the dishes. The house was still very hot, and Norman and I had been hurrying with the kitchen work so we could have a long walk to the park before bed. For once I wasn't completely glad to stop my own life and talk with her. Lois said that Hugh has taken a part-time job in a florist shop owned by a friend of theirs. No reading or writing involved. He works in the back room, with the flowers. He helps to unload the delivery trucks and to keep the various display coolers stocked, and he has learned enough to make arrangements for special orders. He likes it, Lois said, and now every night in addition to himself he brings her a few flowers.

As I listened, I was obliged to enlarge my ongoing picture story of Lois and Hugh to include a daily flower ceremony. I could almost smell their bedecked rooms, their bedroom particularly, the renewable nuptial chamber. It wasn't jealousy, I think, but I did see their lives acutely for a few minutes. I could imagine being Lois, remade every day, every night by sharp issues of love and dismay. She receives the flowers, she chooses to put them in water. Being Hugh, too, fallen into an unlettered and sweet-smelling job. He is handed physical imperfection, he chooses continuance inside an enormous universe, from which there is, anyway, no exit. For a few minutes, still listening to Lois's voice, I felt that I could be anyone, doing anything. My own chosen work had never seemed to me so random, my whole life, my childhood, my marriage, the house on Brentwood Avenue, my plans for the summer, the garden, the fence, our grandchildren, Mother's boxes, new books next fall, all my various desires. And what were my desires anyway? At the moment they seemed suspended.

After Lois and I hung up, I called to Norm that we could still have time for the park if we left right away. My voice sounded like the one I usually hear. As I went to the bathroom and then put on my shoes, everything seemed fairly ordinary. Walking along residential streets with Norman between nine and ten o'clock at night was something I had done thousands of times. We talked a little bit, about this and that. It was easy not to say too much. The air felt good on my bare legs. When we got into the park we slowed down to enjoy the winding walks, the deep shadows, the layer after layer of spaced trees. At the children's playground Norman surprised me by asking if I wanted to swing. When was the last time we had been on swings?

We each took a wooden seat, side by side, gripped the chains, and pumped up to a nice height, and I was having that typical experience of leaving a sensate phantom of my innards hovering in midair each time I arced back into gravity. It was familiar, too, how the visible horizon of housetops and treetops rocked all around us like a great boat in gentle waters. We were in the boat. Finally we stopped pumping, first Norm and then I, and let ourselves become slowing pendulums. It was somewhere in those moments, when I wasn't doing anything, just holding my feet up clear of the well-worn ground and keeping my eyes on the swinging world, that I had an absolute feeling of being complete, and completely myself, right there. This is the something that happened to me. I said to myself, There are no obstacles, and I really didn't know what I meant. It was a very nice feeling. I had no desire, I thought, to talk about it because it felt sufficient in itself, but almost immediately after I stood up I said to Norman that I felt like myself—really like myself, I said—and he said, Well, well, not overly impressed—he sounded just like himself—and I thought of Dexter Thornton's grandfather expelling little plosive breaths and then saying, So it goes, so it goes.

. . .

Another afternoon is done. Workbooks corrected. Orchestra gone home. The sky is darkening toward the rain the garden has been needing all week. As I lift the old metal-framed window panels closed, keeping the chains clear, turning down the latch, I am surprised by the large calmness in me. It is like seeing the wind and hearing the wind, knowing the wind, from a windless place. A soft-skinned child might feel this way, I think, when all wants have been temporarily filled.

I turn out the classroom lights. I have been in this school many years, in one room or another. Life has had business with me, and I guess I must have been doing the plain work of it, all along.

No one else in this upper corridor. Dimness. The distant sounds of outside life. My footfalls. Doorways, rooms, a sequence of rooms to the ninth grade, which is as far as we go here. At the doorway to Social Studies I feel cause to stop. Why? The room is empty, desks empty, blackboard blank. Still I stay near the doorway, corridor side. I breathe the way a child might, just rising out of sleep. What I see is solidly there, a solid empty room, objects spaced in emptiness, with windows like the ones in my room, beyond them a mound of trees, almost like a green hill glimpsed against gray sky, no, just a mound of trees waving in the wind, rain on the way, a quiet room here: and then I know that my vision is of my own death, not as it will one day be in its intricate reality in the world, but as it already is inside me, small, whole, perfect like a seed, not unrecognizable after all, but looking pretty much like another version of life. It must have been here from the beginning.

A NOTE ABOUT THE AUTHOR

Susan Engberg was born and raised in Dubuque, Iowa. She graduated from Lawrence University in Appleton, Wisconsin. In addition to her two prior collections of short stories, her fiction has appeared in several literary publications, including *Prize Stories: The O. Henry Awards* and *The Pushcart Prize VI*. In 1987 she received a Creative Writing Fellowship from the National Endowment for the Arts. She lives with her husband, an architect, in Milwaukee, and they have two daughters.

This book was set in Fournier, a type face named for Pierre Simon Fournier, a celebrated type designer in eighteenth-century France. Fournier's type is considered transitional in that it drew its inspiration from the old style yet was ingeniously innovational, providing for an elegant yet legible appearance. For some time after his death in 1768, Fournier was remembered primarily as the author of a famous manual of typography and as a pioneer of the point system. However, in 1925, his reputation was enhanced when The Monotype Corporation of London revived Fournier's roman and italic.

Composed by Crane Typesetting Service, Inc.,
West Barnstable, Massachusetts

Printed and bound by Fairfield Graphics,
Fairfield, Pennsylvania

Designed by George J. McKeon